THE UNKINDEST CUT

Recent Titles by Gerald Hammond from Severn House

COLD IN THE HEADS
CRASH
DOWN THE GARDEN PATH
THE DIRTY DOLLAR
A DOG'S LIFE
FINE TUNE
THE FINGERS OF ONE FOOT
FLAMESCAPE
GRAIL FOR SALE
HIT AND RUN
THE HITCH
INTO THE BLUE
KEEPER TURNED POACHER
LOVING MEMORY
ON THE WARPATH
THE OUTPOST
A RUNNING JUMP
SILENT INTRUDER
THE SNATCH
THE UNKINDEST CUT
WAKING PARTNERS
WELL AND GOOD
WITH MY LITTLE EYE

THE UNKINDEST CUT

Gerald Hammond

This first world edition published 2012
in Great Britain and in the USA by
SEVERN HOUSE PUBLISHERS LTD of
9–15 High Street, Sutton, Surrey, England, SM1 1DF.
Trade paperback edition first published
in Great Britain and the USA 2013 by
SEVERN HOUSE PUBLISHERS LTD.

British Library Cataloguing in Publication Data

Hammond, Gerald, 1926–
  The unkindest cut.
  1. Highsmith, Jane (Fictitious character) – Fiction.
  2. Fellowes, Ian (Fictitious character) – Fiction.
  3. Scotland – Fiction. 4. Detective and mystery stories.
  I. Title
  823.9'14-dc23

ISBN-13: 978-0-7278-8177-9 (cased)
ISBN-13: 978-1-84751-443-1 (trade paper)

All Severn House titles are printed on acid-free paper.

Severn House Publishers support The Forest Stewardship Council [FSC],
the leading international forest certification organisation. All our titles that
are printed on Greenpeace-approved FSC-certified paper carry the FSC logo.

MIX
Paper from
responsible sources
FSC® C018575

Typeset by Palimpsest Book Production Ltd.,
Falkirk, Stirlingshire, Scotland.
Printed and bound in Great Britain by
MPG Books Ltd., Bodmin, Cornwall.

ONE

Jane Highsmith and Roland Fox had long been neighbours in Birchgrove, a hamlet which consisted of a cluster of small houses designed for first-time buyers, near the southern fringe of Newton Lauder, a little town south of Edinburgh and close to the boundary between moorland and the fertile plain of the Scottish Borders. The pair had started out as friendly neighbours who bade each other good morning or evening and occasionally shared a glass of wine together at convivial moments. Their relationship had progressed slowly, mainly as a result of Roland's sudden realization that he found Jane extremely attractive and had begun looking forward to bumping into her during the day – and he had even engineered the odd meeting if he was honest with himself. So, once he'd made the decision that he wanted something more from their neighbourly relationship, he made his feelings clear and managed to win Jane round to the same way of thinking.

They then spent a few pleasant years enjoying a happy and far from platonic relationship until what had been Jane's family home fell to her on the departure of her older sister Violet, together with her husband, to take up a joint post in Dublin. Violet was a skilled perspective artist while her husband was an equally skilled architectural model maker. Their skills, which complemented each other, led to their being headhunted by the architects to a huge and continuing project. This relieved the stress of a long-term sibling war. The house, Whinmount, was a spacious and solitary but comfortable old house on a byroad that came off the B-road east from Newton Lauder and led almost nowhere that anybody gave a damn about, through farmland and birch woods and heath.

It was a pleasantly secluded and rural location. In summer, when the deciduous trees were in leaf, they had cloistered privacy with only the occasional dog walker or passing car to disturb them. However, in winter, when only the conifers stood up dark against the bright countryside, they could see the roofs of Newton Lauder, the fields around and the moors above. So they had the desired privacy, but company, if wanted, was never too far away.

With Jane inheriting the house, it would, they decided, be a good time to marry. Despite this pragmatic approach to the topic of marriage and lifelong commitment, Jane made clear that she still expected to be 'proposed to' in the traditional way. Since both her parents had long since died, and her great-grandfather GG had passed away a few years ago, there was no one to ask for the permission of her hand in marriage – and she certainly was not going to allow Roland to extend that responsibility to her sister Violet or her husband – but she still wanted to be actually asked, which was fair enough really despite how emancipated she felt. So, Roland good-naturedly did the deed one beautiful spring day, soon after they'd moved into Whinmount, whilst out on an early-morning walk. They were both suitably attired for such an activity in their wellies and Barbour jackets, but on such a dew-soaked morning Roland's right trouser knee got very damp as a result of the obligatory position he'd crouched in whilst popping the all-important question. Needless to say, Jane accepted with a tear in her eye and they could move on to the next phase of their lives.

These lives of theirs were swiftly progressing in the right direction: Jane was in the process of taking over the local veterinary practice, her own smaller set-up having far outgrown its humble beginnings; Roland's second novel had been accepted for publication; they would have the two small houses to let; and Jane had begun to suspect that she might be pregnant. They managed to ignore the other side of the coin – that Jane had had to find a substantial sum for the purchase of the practice while Roland would not see more than a cautious advance against the earnings of his book for more than a year ahead. However, Roland's other source of income was as amanuensis and rewrite-man to his friend and fellow writer, Simon Parbitter. Jane also had money to come from the sale of a Raeburn picture that she had inherited with the house, but the sale was taking its time. 'You can't hurry these things if you want full value,' she was told over and again. And the experts were still arguing as to whether the Raeburn was genuine or 'school of'. The truth, Roland suspected, was that it was, as usual, a bit of both.

As in recent times, the philosophy of the moment was that if you waited for something until you could afford it you would still be awaiting it on your deathbed. With the Micawberish optimism of the comparatively young they knew for a fact that British law would not permit them to starve. Tomorrow was always a lovely day. The sword of Damocles might have hung by a chain rather than a thread.

A wedding need not be expensive, they told each other. A few pounds to the local registrar, a notice in the local rag and the job's done.

So they thought.

They had reckoned without the many locals who they had not realized were also their friends. Roland might be a comparative newcomer but he was well known and well liked and Jane's great-grandfather had been a much loved local citizen, especially by the ladies. Much of his popularity had rubbed off on Jane, who had lived her whole life in the town and, having a sunny temperament and an obliging nature, made friends galore. As soon as the news spread about their impending nuptials, they found that large numbers of the locals not only wanted to know when the event was to take place but expected to be invited to it. A stronger-minded couple might have returned from their honeymoon to present the locality with a fait accompli, but they were not so cunning or practical.

Help was at hand. Not financial help – there was not a surplus of money in the neighbourhood and they were too proud to accept handouts from wealthier friends except in one or two very special circumstances. But Roland and Jane had each been living a shoestring existence, supplementing their meager incomes with what they could grow or shoot or catch by rod, or sometimes, it must be admitted, abstract overnight from the well-filled gardens of others. They had also brought to a fine art the claiming from supermarkets at cut-throat prices the goods that were within a few hours of passing their sell-by dates. So they were, on the whole, well versed in the art of being creatively economic with what they could afford.

Jane, as a veterinary assistant, had been well known and liked by the animal owners round about. She was popular with the locals of her generation – she had been at school with most of them. She was nice-looking, pretty verging on beautiful, and she had a ready laugh with a turn of wit that made her welcome in most company. She had given unstinting service, especially to farmers, and was admired and respected by all she came into contact with in her professional role as the local vet. Consequently, the pair received many offers of meat or vegetables as gifts or at silly prices towards the accumulation of the wedding feast. The chef at the local hotel was one of the few people who could afford to feed a Great Dane on scraps left by the clientele and Jane had nursed the huge dog through a crisis of pyometra. He offered to cook the wedding breakfast for them. And so it went on.

Jane was offered the loan of a half-dozen wedding dresses, one of which was bound to fit her. Jane went by invitation to Hay Lodge, the most opulent house for miles around, to try one on. She dreaded the prospect of not liking the dress on offer, worried it was going to be some frumpy, overly ruffled and lacey Victorian concoction, but she needn't have concerned herself about that. The fit was perfect and the dress was fit for a duchess with a delicately gathered corset on the top half and opulently hooped skirt on the bottom. It was certainly vintage, but so timeless in its intricate design and style that no prospective bride could possibly turn down the chance of wearing such a piece of finery.

'I'll be almost scared to wear it,' she told Mrs Ilwand, the owner of the house and previous wearer of the dress in question.

'Nonsense,' said the lady briskly, running her hand over the ivory silk with obvious pleasure. 'I know you'll take good care of it or I wouldn't be lending it to you. My grandmother was married in it and so was my mother and so was I, but I'll never have a daughter now and you were very good to me whenever any of my menagerie had to be put down. It's the least I can do.'

'Two dogs and a cat,' Jane said, laughing. 'Big deal! But I will be careful. I really appreciate your generosity – it's such a beautiful dress . . .'

'The pet you have at any particular time is invariably special. You were always a great comfort, knowing just the right thing to say.' Mrs Ilwand gave the dress one last loving stroke and handed it over with just a hint of regret in her eyes; more for the lack of her own daughter to wear it than any regret at offering it to her, Jane hoped.

Problems seemed to be solving themselves, but one of the largest obstacles was the subject of alcohol. Their chance of buying champagne for such a crowd of people was, at best, nil. However, Jane was a lady of many talents. She could shoot as well as most men, ride a horse or a bicycle, speak tolerable French and, if the situation justified it, swear. She did a lot of swearing around that time.

None of her other talents was required at the moment; but, almost forgotten, was a knack of making excellent wines including in particular an elderflower champagne that was often voted at least as good as the genuine article. Newton Lauder was favoured in that the countryside suited the elder tree, *Sambucus nigra,* which spread and formed whole areas of woodland behind the hospital. The snag was that there would be no elderflowers until almost the longest day. Roland had had it in mind to marry just before the end of the tax year, thus obtaining tax relief for the whole of the year just past, but simple calculation proved that neither of them would be liable for much, if any, tax for the current year. So June the twentieth became fixed, which gave them a few months to solve the other associated problems.

The entire project would have become impossible and the couple might have been forced to return to the simpler format that they had first envisaged, except that there was a ready-made source of facilities almost on their doorstep.

Mrs Ilwand's father, Sir Peter Hay, a wealthy benefactor of the whole area, had been much concerned about the lack of facilities to lead the up-and-coming generation away from mischief and into what he called 'creative adventure'. With the changes to modern agriculture favouring larger units, small farms were being joined with neighbours and some groups of farm buildings were becoming redundant. Sir Peter had founded Kempfield in what had been the farm of that name and had bequeathed the buildings to the community. The activities that had germinated there had been dictated by a combination of the demand, exemplified by the desires of the young and not so young of the town and environs, and the availability of an experienced professional to give a lead in each subject.

The late Luke Grant, great-grandfather to Jane and her

sister Violet, was always known to the girls as GG for short, and in the reasonless way that such things happen, he had become generally known by that abbreviation. GG had been an early and enthusiastic supporter of Kempfield and on his death Jane had taken over his seat on the management committee and the leadership both of the photographic section and of several projects devoted to the care and training of animals.

Once the seed was sown, Kempfield had continued to grow. A building contractor, Lance Kemnay, had discovered that theft and vandalism on his building sites had almost vanished now that the young could find something better to do with their time and so he had become an enthusiastic supporter, always willing to help out with gifts of materials or help with labour. This bread that he cast on the waters returned manifold because in the process of preparing and extending Kempfield and other buildings that fell to them many youngsters discovered in themselves a knack for some aspect of the building industry and the contractor had found that he had a source of keen, talented and well-behaved apprentices. This in turn appeased the local union representatives who might otherwise have damned the whole project.

Thus, Jane, and Roland with her, had access to a pool of friendly and energetic help with premises to use. While they waited for the elder trees to blossom they had plenty to occupy them. Contrary to male misconceptions, weddings do not organize themselves. They still had their livings to earn. And while elder buds prepared to pop into blossom they had to gather up all the other materials.

Premises entailed much work but little difficulty. By good luck a house on Moorfoot Reservoir was purchased by a family who had no particular use for the boathouse but whose eldest son was desperate to refurbish his vintage Norton motorcycle. There was a section at Kempfield, headed by a retired panel beater, devoted to vehicle restoration; the section devoted to building and sailing racing dinghies moved out to Moorfoot and volunteers began a major clean out of the former boatbuilding workshop.

After the elderflowers, when they ripened, the rest of the materials were readily obtainable. The tools were a different matter. Winemaking kits were on the market by the dozen but not on the scale required. Approaches to the British wine industry were discouraging; evidently, competition was not to be welcomed. A local dairy had recently converted from churns to tanks and would be delighted to lend them stainless steel churns with tight-fitting lids and clamps, but tanks . . . no.

It was not in Jane's nature to admit defeat. Approach enough people and one of them will have what you want; that at least was her philosophy.

TWO

Before buying the small but established veterinary practice, Jane had made many friends by treating, in her kitchen, sick animals beloved by the towns-folk. However, now she had set her face against perpetuating the sharing of her kitchen with such informal veterinary practice. Most clients were accustomed to bringing ill or injured animals to Mr Hicks's clinic and, reluctant though she was to saddle herself with a rent which, though modest by today's standards, would be quite a burden on her stretched finances, Jane could not be confident that her purchase of the goodwill and the client list would necessarily compel the clientele to transfer their loyalty. As part of the deal for taking over the vet's practice on that individual's retirement, therefore, she had taken over his rented surgery in the town square.

Habits, once formed, by their nature tend to persist. Most of the former clients had continued to visit the same address and contact the same phone number and, of those, most seemed delighted to escape her grumpy and abrasive prede-cessor. It seemed that many of these were in the habit of settling their bills in cash and Jane was pleasantly surprised to find that the reported fee income on which, in accord-ance with custom, the purchase price had been based, had been depressed for tax reasons – a practice that she was pleased to continue. This seemed to be generally under-stood. The philosophy of tax evasion had been brought to a fine art by the thrifty Scots.

The surgery, so called, was still in its original form, with a shop where clients might wait and where simple treatments were given, and then a small back room, now with floor and walls tiled, where veterinary surgery could be performed up to a certain level, anything very major being referred to a larger practice in Coldstream or to Edinburgh. On one or two occasions when action had been urgently required, Jane had performed quite major operations in the back room, fortunately with satisfactory results.

A long seat occupied the back wall of the outer room and clients in general rarely had any objection to their animal receiving minor treatment in full view of anyone waiting there for attention and instead enjoyed a sociable exchange of gossip and a discussion of their pets' symptoms, treatment and progress. But the town was growing and Jane accepted that larger premises would soon be necessary; however, for the moment this would suffice very well.

On a day in May, a month or so before the wedding day, Mr Calder, one of the proprietors of the local gun and fishing tackle shop, had called in for a prescription for his Labrador. Keith Calder was a man now well into his sixties. His black hair was thinning and silvered, his face was becoming lined and his step was losing its spring, but he had retained his attractiveness and Jane felt a quite pleasurable loosening of the knees whenever their eyes met. He, being a writer on gun dog subjects among his other interests, was one of the clients who would be claiming his expenditure before tax and she was careful to accept his credit card and to give him a receipt.

He was in no hurry to leave and her next client was still trying to fit a large car into a small parking space in the Square. He leaned on the counter. 'I've seen you with a young Labrador,' he said. It was as much a question as a statement.

Jane nodded. 'Sheba,' she said. 'Her paternal grandfather was your Briesland Echo.'

'She should be all right then. Echo's strain has been

sound. Do you work her? You seemed to be training her
as a worker the other day. I've seen you with a dummy
launcher.'

'She's young enough yet,' Jane said. 'I'd like to give
her some work in the not too distant future.'

'We're looking for another picker-up. I'll phone you.'

Jane felt a glow of pleasure. Anyone with two legs
capable of independent movement can be a beater but to
be invited to 'pick up' on a shoot, and presumably even
to be paid a pittance for it, equates with acceptance as a
competent dog trainer with a trustworthy dog.

'That would be great, but the family may make it impossible for another year.' She patted her midriff. She was
showing very little but Keith would have been aware of
her pregnancy through Deborah, his daughter and Jane's
friend.

Keith snorted in answer which could have meant
anything from derision at a good picker-upper going to
waste or congratulations on her news. Knowing Keith it
was probably the former, Jane acknowledged, but she
didn't mind and was still grateful for the old man's offer
and was keen to take him up on it as soon as the situation
allowed.

As Keith left, another patient arrived, this one dripping
a little blood on the PVC tiles. Dog and owner were taken
into the back room and Jane got to work. After stitching a
wound in the leg of Stella – or possibly Stellar, nobody
was quite sure – she found that the previous first patient in
line had still not yet arrived, its owner having dented somebody else's car in the car park and got into an argument
about insurance. Jane could see figures gesticulating out in
the Square, no doubt trying to work out who was to blame
with neither party admitting to an apology. Meanwhile,
back in the surgery, Jane was chatting to Lance Kemnay,
the owner of the ridgeback Stella whose leg she'd just
stitched up. Lance was the local helpful contractor and

patron of Kempfield. He was a burly man with a blue chin, full lips and a surprisingly deep voice. He had begun his working life as a joiner but his wife had had a win with a premium bond. Instead of blowing it on a world cruise they had set him up as a building contractor, and in the ensuing dozen or so years he had won and carried out successive building contracts of escalating value without putting a foot wrong and without making any extravagant claims for extras. Developers were clamouring for his services.

Jane and Lance had settled down for a chat over a cup of machine tea, Lance seated in the one bentwood chair reserved for the client at the head of the queue while Jane leaned on the counter. That day there was no queue. Lance had no grounds to claim Stella's costs before tax so he paid cash. He had been playing hooky from business, he explained, decoying pigeon on his cousin's farm until Stella had gashed herself on broken glass. He was usually well dressed but that day he was wearing tweed breeks and an old sweater.

'How go the preparations for the Feeding of the Five Thousand?' he asked.

She knew that the question was a polite formality but it was at the front of her mind so she told him anyway. 'Pray God it doesn't turn out to be that many but it seems to be heading in that direction. We've been promised most of the consumables,' she said, 'by which I mean food, and a small working party of mothers is turning the raw materials into a buffet with the help and supervision of the chef at the hotel. Mrs Ilwand is lending me a gorgeous wedding dress. The meal will have to be a stand-up buffet. Drink is the remaining problem. Everything else seems to be providing itself but the booze is different and I haven't dared to count the number of people who're expecting invitations. I've been advised to tell people to bring their own or else to give them one glass of sherry and then leave them to pay for their own, but you can't *do* that. So we timed it to catch the elderflower season and I'm going to make a superginormous batch of my elderflower champagne. And if anybody turns up their nose at that—'

'They won't,' Lance said, laughing. Jane's elderflower champagne was famous and much respected throughout the district.

'Well, if they do, *then* they can bloody well fetch their own from the off-licence.' Jane went on to recount the lengths that they were going to in order to brew the required quantity of wine.

When she mentioned her need of a stainless steel tank, Lance sat up suddenly. 'I have just what you want,' he said. 'You probably saw that the extension to the athletic centre in Edinburgh was cancelled. I had already put some materials on order. Most of them I managed to absorb into other work but there was a tank that was intended for the boiler room – something to do with sterilization of swimming pool water with the use of ozone – that nobody wanted. I got paid for it anyway but I was left with it on my hands. I didn't know whether to send it to the dump or cut it up for bits and pieces.'

'Don't do either of those, one of them could be the answer to a maiden's prayer. Not that I could claim to be a maiden,' Jane said, stroking her stomach where she was convinced that the bump was becoming noticeable at her waist, although to the untrained eye it looked as taut as ever.

Lance laughed. 'I damn nearly said that I see what you mean, but I just managed to stop myself in time and actually I can't really notice a thing! Anyway, congratulations. That's great news for you and Roland. Now,' Lance continued, this time in a more serious tone, but with a smile on his lips, 'getting back to the business at hand, regarding the tank, I'll send Mrs Stiggs over in the morning. She'll take you over there.'

'Thank you – and regarding the matter at hand,' Jane

replied, being equally businesslike and with her own smile playing round her mouth, 'I do know my way to your warehouse.'

'Not this one you don't. It used to be a church hall until I built them the newer and better one. So this is a different place and it's much easier if I just send Mrs Stiggs over to take you there tomorrow instead of having to give you complicated directions, which you'll then lose and will phone me up in a panic totally lost, no doubt. No, this is much the easiest solution all round. And, out of the good-ness of my heart and because I want to be rid of the tank, I'll even transport it for you. That pickup that they use for Kempfield would hardly look at it.'

Jane, who had been expecting to have to use relays of milk churns, had switched to expecting a need to do some-thing clever with a boat trailer, but now she could relax. 'Write down your name complete with your middle names,' Jane said. 'I'm going to nominate you for a JCB in the next honours list.'

Lance tried to laugh with his mouth full of tea. It was lucky that he was wearing older clothes than usual. 'I'll see that you get it back in good order,' Jane said, mopping up the spillage with a paper towel.

'But I don't *want* it back,' Lance insisted, mopping his eyes with a swab provided by Jane. 'That's the whole point. I'm trying to get rid of it. Take it away and lose it, for all I care.'

'Then you wouldn't mind if I made holes for immersion heaters in it?'

'I'll say this again for the last time. Watch my lips, Jane. I . . . do . . . not . . . want . . . it . . . back. If you try to give it back to me I shall drop it on your foot.'

'Then the yacht group can cut it up for chainplates and things when I've finished with it. That wasn't a question,' Jane added hastily. 'I was summarizing.'

*　　*　　*

Next morning Mrs Stiggs telephoned to find which part of Jane's day was unencumbered by surgery times and duly turned up with another driver and Lance's Audi. Vets have to drive a lot of miles and Jane had only been able to afford a Citroën 2CV and not a very new one, so to be driven in a quiet and comfortable car was a luxurious novelty. In the surgery window Jane hung the sign that she kept for these occasions. Neatly printed by computer and duly laminated, it read: 'CALLED AWAY. IN EMERGENCY PHONE . . .' and there followed the eleven digits of her mobile phone number. A similar message went on to her answering machine.

In the nearby jeweller's shop, just a few doors along the Square, a local young woman called Helen Maple, who considered herself to be the local female factotum, was in charge for the moment but not heavily occupied, so Jane asked her to look out for disappointed customers Helen happened to notice lingering outside the surgery, most probably looking for dog food, flea powder or biscuits. Helen was happy to oblige and Jane was free to go.

Mrs Stiggs was a widow, slightly overweight but still not without her sex appeal because she gave her face, figure and hair the intense care that an infatuated owner gives to a garden. She was a good driver but on this occasion, because of a sprained ankle, her daughter Joyce had come along as driver. Joyce, who was red haired, blue eyed and slender, also took a pride in her personal appearance. She was very well dressed in colours suited to her strong complexion and a summer dress cut to flatter her slightly plump figure. She, like her mother, worked for Lance Kemnay, though in a more junior position.

Jane hopped in the back seat of the Audi, luxuriating in the plump leather seats and ample leg room. It was only a short fifteen-minute journey, but Jane revelled in this time out from her busy day; it was a great excuse to take her rather aching feet out of her shoes (as sensible as they were for a vet) and massage the soles of her feet and her ankles, both of which were beginning to suffer under the strain of slight water retention and extra weight.

Joyce conveyed them all, briskly but safely, to the former church hall at Longdene. Once the expedition members had exited the car, both Jane and Mrs Stiggs showing signs of stiffness, they entered the building, negotiated their way around piles of various building materials and sacks of cement and there, half hidden by a stack of terrazzo floor tiles, was a tank. It looked more than large enough.

'How many glasses of champagne would that hold, do you think?' Jane asked.

Lance retained the services of Mrs Stiggs as his secretary at the cost of a substantial salary, not for her looks but because she was the sort of person who knew the contents of the average champagne glass in cubic centimetres, could estimate the dimensions of the tank by eye and could divide the one by the other in her head. She had hobbled from the car with the aid of two sticks but her mind was still needle sharp. 'Just under a hundred and twenty thousand,' she said.

That sounded rather a lot but they need not fill the tank to the brim and Jane was not going to pass up the chance of a free stainless steel tank. 'I should think that'll do it,' she said. 'Please tell Mr Kemnay to go ahead, shift it to Kempfield and to let me know when it's coming. Or going. Or whatever. And ask him where those terrazzo tiles are destined for. We could use them at Kempfield.' Jane knew that when a contract included terrazzo floor tiles the contractor would usually allow for a spare quantity because if extra was needed the first run would be almost impossible to match for colour. So consequently he very often ended up with the surplus on his hands.

Mrs Stiggs winked. 'Leave it with me. I'll see to it.'

Joyce, however, did not approve of Lance's frequent

gifts to Kempfield. 'They should be paying for all these materials,' she said defiantly.

'What do you care?' her mother asked rather tartly. 'It doesn't come out of your pocket.'

'I suppose not,' Joyce said doubtfully.

Mrs Stiggs and Jane exchanged raised brows and subtle yet amused smiles and all concerned made their way back to Newton Lauder, Jane now that much closer to a completely organized wedding.

There were some clients whose animals Jane had treated, at least once in the past, without looking for payment. These were those whose favours she was likely to need on some other occasion. Among them was an impecunious farmer who had woken her from a deep sleep when he thought, mistakenly, that his cattle had eaten a poisonous weed. From him she called in her favour and demanded the loan of a tractor, trailer and driver on a date chosen after careful scrutiny of the calendar and the weather. Other tradesmen and shopkeepers had been blarneyed or blackmailed into providing goods or services as well.

However, Jane had no need to use blackmail on the young members at Kempfield. For many of them she had nursed a sick puppy or kitten back to health or had obtained special access to facilities at Kempfield or elsewhere. The page posted in the lobby for members volunteering to pick elderflowers soon had to be supplemented with extra pages. A plumber whose son's budgerigar's talons she had clipped had, in return, fitted and connected immersion heaters to the tank.

This enthusiasm to help her out just proved that Jane was a very well-liked and popular member of the local community and how, as a prominent person on the committee of Kempfield, she had earned the respect and friendship of many of the young who frequented the place. GG had also been incredibly well respected in his role as photography course leader, and many of the now respectable thirty-somethings of Newton Lauder owed their present success to GG's role as their mentor which had kept them from veering into the world of the petty criminal.

On the day chosen for the big elderflower pick, the tractor and trailer made four runs between Kempfield and two stretches of woodland rich in elder trees. A measured quantity of water had been added to the tank and brought to the required temperature. The elderflower heads were added, together with lemon, wine vinegar and bags of sugar. Two boys who had been prevented, by leg injuries incurred in a football match, from joining the harvesting party were left to stir the concoction which was then covered with muslin, and the tank was wrapped in insulating material and left.

The yeast that was working itself up in a clean jar proved unnecessary – after two days the tank could be heard and smelled from anywhere in the complex. All activities involving paints or anything else that might taint the wine had already been banned. For four more days the brew was left to bloop and gurgle. Then it was siphoned through muslin filters into milk churns, the lids were clamped down and additionally fastened with fencing wire, the room allowed to cool and the churns left to finish their fermentation in peace. The tank was scrubbed out and went to store.

The date for the wedding was coming close but, while the ceremony was of interest only to the young female members of the fashion and catering sections, the male members foreswore their boats, cars, motorcycles, furniture and firearms for a period and turned their attention to Kempfield itself. The project had sparked the general imagination and the reception was to be the success of the century or else . . .

THREE

In addition to those who loved Jane or owed her favours, somehow the idea of this wedding above all others being the one occasion for everybody to meet and greet had caught on and spread like flu. Even the Newton Lauder Hotel ballroom would not have contained the crowd that was expected for what would undoubtedly be the wedding of the decade, but the former barns and cattle courts of Kempfield had ample space. They had been scrubbed out, lined, decorated and redecorated several times since being taken over and could be made available at short notice. Two hectic days were spent on another clean and a clearance of the three largest workshops and then some clever work with cheerful wrapping paper completed the transformation, disguising the utilitarian spaces as circus tents. Most of the problems were resolved by intelligent analysis but the removal and storing of machinery made demands on the pure manpower which, fortunately, was available. Jane's own attitude vacillated between trepidation and eager anticipation.

While all that work was going on, Jane was checking over her mental list and ticking off the jobs to be done. Surely everything was almost done . . . Then, on her very wedding eve, it hit her, forming such a distraction that she nearly inoculated a Persian cat against brucellosis. She was so used to driving herself everywhere that her mental picture had faded away at the point of getting herself from place to place apparently by teleportation. Guests could be trusted to make their own ways to Kempfield; and if they became unfit to drive and had to walk home again at least it was downhill all the way for the locals. The bride, however, would be expected to arrive and depart with dignity. A phone call established that nobody had remembered to book the limousine kept at the Ledbetters' garage and service station which was generally reserved for weddings and funerals and the occasional visit of a VIP.

To her infinite relief, the limousine was still available. A few minutes later, responding to her phone call, Alistair Ledbetter arrived at the surgery by motorbike, hoping to settle the details of the booking. He was Mr Ledbetter's second son and, in Jane's opinion, a few litres short of a gallon; but he was a handsome boy, a good driver and he kept the limo shining like a mirror. On the whole, the limousine driving was his responsibility and the rest of his days were spent polishing the limo, doing odd jobs around the garage or vanishing to take his amusement elsewhere. If he sometimes made advances to the occasional unaccompanied bride on the way to the church, or the odd visiting female VIP, nobody had complained yet.

'Thought we'd be hearing from you, one of these days,' he said. 'What time do you want picked up?'

They discussed times and places. There was nobody to give the bride away and because she had been living with the groom for two years such an attendant had seemed superfluous. Deborah Calder was to act as Maid of Honour and would be collected from her own home by the limousine as well.

For once, Alistair was anxious to be helpful. He was looking hangdog, which was not his usual expression. 'Can't lend me a hundred quid, I suppose?' he enquired, once the formalities of the booking had been gone through and he was about to zoom off on his motorbike.

Alistair was known to gamble. Jane had heard it said that to repay a loan was against his religion. 'If I could,' she said, 'I'd lend it to myself. Try your father.'

Alistair made a sound that combined contempt with

derision. 'Not a hope. And don't you go telling him I asked.' He drove off.

Jane, who had been short of money for years, hated to hear of anyone else in that predicament, but Alistair had left and Jane's attention had to be given to her newly arrived patient's owners, Mary Kemp and Jolene Henderson. The two ladies lived together but, as was well known, they were certainly not lesbians. They were an artist and an artists' model. Jolene had seen a mouse so they had accepted the gift of a kitten from a neighbour who had spurned Jane's offer to neuter her tabby cat and was paying the price. Now they had brought it in for its shots and to be microchipped. There were no other clients waiting so Jane decided against bothering to transfer to the back room where anything smacking of surgery was usually performed. Jane did the job to the loud indignation of the little feline and replaced the plastic syringe on the shelf below the counter.

Among the ladies of Newton Lauder, Jane's wedding was the only subject to be discussed with her – or, usually, with each other. 'Where are you going for your honeymoon?' Jolene asked. 'Or is it a secret?'

'It's a secret from me,' Jane said. 'We're both snowed under with work. I can't get a locum until September and Roland's promised to do some more editing for Simon Parbitter but his own publisher is making noises about his next book and the film director wants changes to the script of Simon's last one.'

Her words were peevish but there was undoubtedly satisfaction in her tone of voice. Before Jane took over the surgery, locals had been inclined to take offence at her predecessor's brusque manner and take their business elsewhere, whereas now, clients from further afield were travelling to her clinics, not only for her veterinary skill, but also her open manner and friendly disposition that made chatting with her such a pleasure.

'At least you're both busy, so you should soon be on Easy Street at last,' said Mary. She smiled her angelic smile. (Mary and Jolene lived mainly on Mary's illustrating of comic books. Mary had an exceptionally beautiful face and head which she used, with subtle changes, for most of her principal female characters. Jolene was rather pug-faced but her figure was superb and carefully tended to ensure that it stayed that way.)

Jane made the sound that is usually reproduced as 'Huh!'. She wrinkled her nose. 'Money tomorrow is never the problem. Money today tends to be in short supply. Hence the expression "Tomorrow never comes".'

'True,' Jolene said. 'Unless you've been dreading it.'

Jane's next appointment, her last as a spinster, was one that she had been dreading and it brushed the smile from her face. It was her sad task to put down an old man's friend, the very old dog who had been his companion for twenty-three years but had now reached the end of the road. She filled the hypodermic syringe with the sleeping draught that she used for the purpose and put on the stethoscope. While the owner held the dog's head and whispered words of comfort she pressed the plunger until the old heart stopped its feeble beating. The old man was in tears. She gave him a comforting hug. 'Anyone who doesn't feel bad at such a time,' she said, 'shouldn't be allowed to keep an animal.' Her own voice was husky but she managed to hold back her tears until the old man was safely on his solitary way.

Despite her words, tomorrow did come: Jane's wedding day and the craziest day of her life. Pandering to the superstition that the groom must never see the bride until they are at the altar, or the registrar's desk, Roland had slept in a spare room and gone out early, intending to don his wedding finery at a friend's house. Jane had scorned the need for a bridesmaid to help her dress and she had allowed an unnecessarily generous margin for getting into an unfamiliar wedding dress, so she was waiting in the hall at Whinmount, nostalgically enjoying the many skilled examples of GG's photographic work that hung on the walls, when the bridal car arrived with Alistair looking very smart at the wheel and the white silk ribbons glowing in the sunshine.

Up to that point the day had gone like clockwork. It was about to go mad. A glance at her watch (the bride's present from the groom) assured her that it was not quite the time for her phone calls to be diverted to another vet twenty miles away, so she was carrying her mobile phone, charged and switched on. She was just getting into the car when it sounded its jingle.

'Injured puppy,' said a voice that she did not recognize. 'It's spouting blood. I'm taking it to your surgery.' The call was cut off. She keyed 1471 but the caller had withheld his number – presumably his phone was kept in that mode.

Jane looked at her watch again. The dilemma seemed to be ripping her mind apart. This was her big moment of her big day. She had wished that GG could have been there to accompany her up the aisle. She wished that Roland was beside her to tell her what to do. But she could not possibly leave a puppy to bleed to death. She would just have time, and in the surgery, if there was a reasonable chance of saving the pup, she could change into the overall that hung in the back room and still get to Kempfield, not more than slightly behind time. It was, after all, the bride's privilege to be late. She grabbed up the surgery keys and seated herself in the back of the big car. 'Take me first to my surgery in the Square,' she told Alistair.

Alistair looked slightly shocked at the unconventional start to a bride's big event, but the authority in Jane's voice, and the fact that she was a paying customer, convinced him to follow her instructions.

As the limo moved off, Jane's phone rang again. This time she knew the voice, which belonged to Lucas Fraine, the Kempfield manager, who was in charge of the organization. Usually blessed with the calm of a traffic policeman she could detect traces of panic in his voice. 'I don't know what you put in that champagne, but we went to open the first churn,' he said, 'just to check that it really had fermented,' – in other words to start the drinking – 'and when we cut the wires – whoosh! – the top blew off, the lid punched a hole in the ceiling tiles and nearly brained John Staples coming down again and there's wine all over the floor and—'

'You were supposed to wait until I was there,' Jane said through gritted teeth. 'I was going to borrow the tarpaulin that we scrubbed up for covering dinghies and use it the way a waiter uses a napkin but on a much bigger scale. We scrubbed it specially. Just do the best you can, hang on and I'll get there as soon as possible. I have an emergency here. Apologize for me.' The call finished.

Jane suddenly realized that they were already entering the Square. A young man was lingering outside her surgery, nursing a wrapped bundle. Otherwise, fortunately, the Square was empty.

'Drop me at the surgery,' she said, 'and then wait in the lane behind the shops. You've got your mobile and it's still on the same number? I'll call you when I'm ready.' She had no wish to attract a crowd.

Alistair nodded his assent to her in the mirror and drove off once Jane had manoeuvred herself and the rather cumbersome wedding dress out of the car. She walked over to the surgery door expectantly.

The young man would still have been in his late teens. Jane remembered seeing him around the town. He was usually smart and clean but just now he was badly blood-stained and obviously very upset. A thin wailing came from inside the bundle. 'I think it was hit by a car,' he said. 'I found it at the roadside and I couldn't think what to do except bring it to the vet.'

'I understand.'

'I forgot you're getting married today. My mum's at your wedding. I'm so sorry if I've messed it up for you.' The boy was in danger of becoming tearful.

'It's all right,' Jane said, unlocking the surgery door. 'I told you I understood and I do. You couldn't have done anything else. I couldn't pass by an injured pup myself. Bring it inside.'

She led the way and cleared a space on the counter. 'Unwrap it for me.' She stood, as she thought, well back.

The pup was wrapped in an old mackintosh. At the first turn of the unwrapping Jane could see that the task was hopeless. 'There's too much damage,' she said. 'No animal, especially a young puppy, could survive that much surgery. Hold him like that. I'll have to put him to sleep.'

'Oh dear! If you say so.' The young man swallowed loudly. 'I've never seen a death.'

She produced the syringe that she had used to release the old dog the day before. It still held more than enough of the sleeping mixture for a small puppy. As she stooped over the pup there was a sudden spurt of blood and the wailing increased. Flustered, she slipped in the needle and gave the merciful dose. The sound died. The pup stretched, shivered and was still.

'It was kindest that way,' Jane said. She looked down at herself. She took animal suffering very seriously and in the stress she had forgotten to change or cover the wedding dress. 'Oh my God, look at me!' The once exquisite ivory lace, dress was now peppered with spots of blood which were rapidly spreading along the tiny threads of the dress as the blood was absorbed into the material. A bloody map of veins had now printed itself across the front of the dress. It was ruined.

'Well, I'm sorry,' said the youth, rather petulantly this time, 'but it wasn't my fault.'

'Never mind whose fault,' Jane said. 'Do you have any money on you?'

'Not a lot.'

'Dash over to the grocer's and get me some salt. Very, very quickly.'

He scampered off outside. Jane could hear his trainers scraping and skidding on the gravel of her small courtyard as he raced out into the Square and over the crossing to the shop on the other side of the road.

Seconds later his figure was replaced by the shadow of another, this one equally slim and in the youthful uniform of jeans and a T-shirt. However, it was soon apparent that this was not the boy returning from his emergency errand, but another person, this one wearing a woollen hat in the colours of the local football team, pulled down over its face; the eyeholes had been cut and neatly hemmed. As the figure loomed closer, Jane could now see it through the glass of her surgery door and noticed with a shock that the person was carrying a kitchen knife, large and sharp-looking. Before Jane had time to react, the person was inside her surgery, the door shut behind them and the latch was dropped. The person then came forward, keeping the knife pointed at Jane's throat. She backed against the counter, trying to edge away from the threat without turning her back on him. There was no way she could get past him to the door to make her escape, so the only action she could take was to try and melt into the background and hope the person would ignore her presence if she didn't draw attention to herself.

The intruder meanwhile produced a carrier bag and using the blade of the knife began to slide drugs off the shelves of the drug cabinet into it. With a sense of relief Jane realized that rape, or any other such nightmare, was not on the agenda.

'Open the safe,' said the voice in a gritty whisper.

'There isn't a safe,' Jane said in tones that had developed a wobble.

The statement was almost true. Among the shopkeepers of Newton Lauder a sort of General Post was quite usual. The surgery had been built as a small shop for a jeweller who had later, as business grew, moved to where Keith Calder and his partner now worked, and then moved again into still larger premises further along the Square. The first occupant, fearing robbery, had caused a box of heavy steel with a slot in the lid to be built beneath the counter and bolted into place. Any takings above the float needed for making change went through the slot and the key was kept at the bank next door but two. That was considered to have averted any danger of robbery for cash. The jeweller's stock, it was generally agreed, was rubbish anyway. Mr Hicks, the vet from whom Jane had bought the practice, had kept the box but replaced the key lock with a digital combination lock. Jane had continued the same system but this was the first robbery to be attempted. There would be little cash inside; she had banked it the previous afternoon. Most of the few accounts since then had been settled by credit card or cheque, but a stubborn part of her mind hated to think of the system failing after so many years.

'Steel box,' ground out the whisperer. 'Open it.' Jane had backed up against the counter. The knife had come so close to her throat that she could read the maker's name.

Jane's mind began to work with almost its normal fluency. 'You'll have to key in four-three-seven-two-six,' she said.

The intruder's reaction was predictable. If the man went round the counter, leaving Jane free in the shop, she would be able to unlatch the door and bolt for it. The intruder instead pushed her ahead round the counter. Then, rather than making her open the box, the burglar stooped to the front of the steel box and as he did so a wide gap opened between the intruder's jeans and T-shirt. Jane reached under the counter and blindly searched along the shelf, trying not to panic, until her hand clasped on to what she'd been looking for and, as she brought her hand slowly back out from under the counter, in her fist she was tightly holding on to a syringe. With a savage swipe she stabbed the burglar somewhere in the vicinity of the left kidney.

Her intention of course had been to use the remainder of the sleeping draught to lay him out. If the amount remaining in the syringe was insufficient to knock him out it would surely have stupefied the intruder enough to allow Jane to make her escape. It was only a second or two later that she realized that she had got hold of the wrong syringe. She dropped it back on to the shelf in disgust.

The burglar froze in the act of stuffing some untidy paper into his pocket. In a slightly more natural but still disguised voice the intruder squawked loudly, then reverted to the hoarse whisper. 'What you done to me?'

Jane pulled herself together. 'I've just microchipped you,' she said bravely. There was a momentary silence broken only when somebody tried the door and, on finding it locked, pushed a small packet of salt through the letter box. Footsteps receded. Silence would only leave the intruder free to think thoughts that Jane would prefer to let die. She picked up the packaging of the syringe from the shelf below the counter. 'If you really want to know, I can even tell you your number.'

The whisper rose in panic. 'Don't be funny. Take the microchip out of me. Quickly, or I'll slice your face off.'

She was in no doubt that the intruder had begun to lose control. Strangely, to be the calmer of the two steadied her nerves. 'I can't,' she said, improvising wildly. 'Nobody could. It's inside one of your kidneys. If it's taken out you'll be on dialysis for the rest of your life, so if you harm me you're already carrying the proof of your guilt.'

The burglar made a half-hearted slash in the direction

of Jane's head. She ducked back and the knife barely missed her scalp. A few strands of dark chestnut hair drifted down. Now the intruder turned and fumbled at the door. It swung open and then slammed shut after the figure left and she heard footsteps scampering away. He had gone; her ordeal was over. Jane was aware how lucky she'd been to have barely had anything stolen aside from some drugs and a small amount of cash. A few moments later, once she was absolutely sure that the intruder had left, never to return, and once the adrenaline had stopped pumping through Jane's body, her emotions took over and she crumpled to the floor in relief and shock at how close she'd been to a far nastier, potentially more harmful experience.

Her mobile phone was already in her hand although she had no recollection of taking it out. She meant to call Alistair but first she called Kempfield. Lucas Fraine answered. She managed to compress the story into an amazing minimum of words and told him again to apologize to everyone and explain. But most importantly to let the groom know she had been delayed at the surgery, so that he didn't start to wonder what was keeping her or worse that he didn't start to consider the possibility that she could be having second thoughts. She promised that she would explain all later. Lucas sounded more upset than she did but she disconnected from his incoherent enquiries after her well-being.

Having somewhat collected her emotions and turned to the more practical issues at hand, she noticed for the first time that there was not a mirror in the place. She began sponging at the wedding dress with a mixture of water and the salt the young boy had delivered through the letter box, but the edges of the bloodstains had by now dried in. When Alistair arrived in answer to her second phone call she said, 'Take me home again. I'll have to change. Quickly.'

Alistair looked in horror at her bloodied dress. 'You're

not allowed to bleed all over my good seats.' It was touching that his concern was for his car upholstery rather than the dishevelled bride.

'I'm not going to bleed anywhere,' Jane said. 'It's not me who's bleeding.'

For some mad reason this seemed to satisfy Alistair. She sprawled on the luxurious back seat and breathed deeply. She felt that it might have relieved her feelings if she could have snarled like a wolf or bitten somebody, but there are few nervous outlets available to a seriously bloodstained bride. She contained herself as they drove up the hill.

FOUR

In the door mirror of the limo she could see herself although there was no comfort in that view. The puppy's blood was not only over the wedding dress, it had sprayed on to her face and hands and was even splattered in her hair. If there had been anybody in the Square they would have been staring, their attention first caught by the reappearance of the bridal car and then the sound of her scampering feet. She pretended to herself that she could make herself invisible, as she had done in moments of embarrassment ever since her childhood, though as far as she knew it had never worked yet.

The limo made short work of the steep hill. Alistair had longed for somebody to ask him to hurry and now was his chance. The fat tyres produced a squeal as he turned off into the byroad. The rest of the trip back to Whinmount passed in a flash. As soon as she leapt out of the car – as fast as the corseted wedding dress would allow – Jane gave instructions to Alistair to go and fetch Deborah, her Maid of Honour. The first thing that Jane saw on darting inside the front door was the light flashing on the recently installed telephone, insisting that there were messages. There was, in fact, a string of messages and they were all from Deborah, desperate to know why she had not been collected yet. Was she forgotten? While trying not to look at herself in the hall mirror, Jane called her Maid of Honour and assured her that the limo was on the way. She told her to sit beside the driver so as not to run the risk of staining whatever gorgeous dress she was no doubt wearing. Rather than be trapped in the hall answering a thousand questions, Jane disconnected.

She collected a big jar of salt and dashed upstairs. The bath was quickly part-filled with water and salt and she left the wedding dress to soak in it, while knowing that it was already far too late. Hoping against hope, she scanned her wardrobe but no miracle had produced a long white dress since the last time that she looked in it. There was nothing all-white except a tennis frock, but that was so short that it would barely have covered her underwear. Then memory threw up an inspiration. She closed the wardrobe and went to the airing cupboard and there she found a white nightdress of some silky material, a present from Roland on a recent birthday and never worn because it was far too sexy even for a fiancée. Perhaps for a husband it might have been just within the bounds of the permissible. As a wedding dress it would be outrageous but of the various choices open to her it seemed the least unacceptable and in fact the only one possible.

In washing the blood off her face Jane had necessarily removed the make-up that she had patiently applied two hours earlier. The return of Alistair brought relief in the form of Deborah, the Maid of Honour, who absorbed the sorry tale and, although her hand was shaking – with laughter Jane hoped – at the thought of the microchipped robber, managed to remove the more obvious bloodstains from Jane's hair and to make a better job of the make-up than Jane herself had managed. With the veil pinned over her hair, Deborah said nobody would ever know that anything was amiss. The fact that the veil would be removed during the ceremony was not mentioned. Deborah directed Alistair's attention to the view over the town while Jane whipped a sheet of polythene out of the house and flipped it over the back seat.

They were still tidying the veil during the short journey to Kempfield, whilst Jane was filling Deborah in on the eventful day so far. Deborah was still firing off a million questions to Jane when Alistair indicated that they were arriving at Kempfield. Jane was mentally unprepared as they swept into the outer courtyard and stopped at the big doors. It was hardly the serene kind of preparation appropriate for a bride just as she's about to make the most important union of her life, but it was the only time Jane was going to get considering they were already running at least fifty minutes late; even the most high-maintenance of brides couldn't expect to keep her groom and congregation waiting any longer.

There had originally been a huge, open inner courtyard between the farm buildings but as the centre grew unstoppably, as well-managed enterprises will, and its catchment area had expanded, this had been roofed over to make an enormous general purpose workshop. It had now been cleared of benches, machinery and ongoing projects and then decorated tastefully but frivolously with garlands of coloured wrapping paper from the printworks, whose manager had been at school with Jane. It was into this building that Jane made her entrance, with Deborah behind her, holding a delightful bouquet of flowers that the local florist had donated, of which there were plenty more in strategic places around the venue.

On making her belated entry to the sound of a great cheer, Jane was stunned by the number present. Somehow news of the event had got a mention on the Internet, probably on Facebook, and in the local media, with a hint that the event was open to any friend of a friend of the bride or her family; and it seemed that this definition might have become stretched almost to snapping point. Champagne had been mentioned without the proviso that it had been made on the spot and from elderflowers rather than grapes, and of course everyone expected a great feast as well.

Looking around, Jane could see officials, volunteer leaders and benefactors of Kempfield; former schoolfellows, fellow students from college; many of GG's old friends, clients and colleagues; her own clients and most of the denizens of

Newton Lauder. It had been made clear that morning suits were not expected; the groom and the best man wore kilts and tweed jackets and at that point formality ended. So the guests were a multicoloured, melting pot of all styles, fashions, uniforms and hairdos; everyone having their own opinion of what constitutes an acceptable dress code at a wedding on a gorgeous summer's day.

While the bride was awaited the festivities had begun anyway and luckily the supplies of food and elderflower champagne seemed to be holding up. It seemed that volunteers had managed to clear up most of the mess of the earlier explosion, but the smell of wine was all-pervading, although considering everyone was drinking the stuff, and would be consuming plenty of it as the day wore on, they would become immune to the smell fairly quickly.

As Jane entered further into the room, she noticed the expressions on various faces – the men entranced, the younger women envious and the older ladies outraged – and was reminded that the nightdress that was now substituting for the bloodied wedding dress was daring in the extreme, being made of a very thin and clinging material with inserts and panels of lace that was so transparent as to be barely visible. Oh well! She would soon be a respectable married woman. And she had been too busy to have the traditional hen night. Surely some allowance could be made. She avoided eye contact with any of the throng as she held her head up and walked calmly forward towards the rear of the room, which was to act as the wedding ceremony area.

Manfred, Jane's soon-to-be brother-in-law, was to be best man. Roland and Manfred were first to reach Jane. Roland in particular was almost gagging with questions and he rushed up to her, clasping her hand in both of his. His expression was a mixture of relief and concern; relief that Jane had turned up (as part of him had begun to worry that she was having second thoughts about their future), and concern at what exactly had delayed her. Manfred too was spouting questions, but Jane hushed them both. She was living in hyperdrive.

'It's not the bride's place to make speeches,' she said. 'Manfred, your job. Please apologize to everybody. Explain. Urgent call surgery. Attempt to rob knifepoint. Microchipped the . . . the intruder. Got blooded, went home to change. Sorry delay. Please enjoy.'

She stood back, confident that she had given a full explanation. Manfred was a tall man with a head of carefully waved hair and a handsome face ruined, in Jane's opinion, by an effeminate mouth. Putting flesh on the bare bones, he began a tolerable speech of explanation and apology.

As Manfred finished, Jane found herself breathing heavily with nothing to do at last except to get married. But before that could happen she was approached by a confused-looking Mrs Ilwand. Emotion flushed over her. Before the other could speak, Jane burst out, 'I'm sorry about your wedding dress, so sorry, but the pup was spouting blood – I had to put it down in the end – I couldn't just leave it. I was going to—'

Mrs Ilwand managed to break in without slapping her and instead held on tightly to her forearms in a half reassuring and half restraining embrace. 'My dear, never mind the bloody dress. I don't have a daughter to pass it on to. I urged you to look after it so that I could give it to a charity shop. I'll make a donation instead. More importantly, are *you* all right? That's the point. I could barely understand what the best man was going on about, but I gather it has something to do with an injured pup and lots of blood . . .?' Mrs Ilwand looked at Jane with a sympathetic tilt of her head and grasped her for another hug.

Jane could have fainted with relief; she couldn't believe that Mrs Ilwand was being so forgiving about the ruined wedding dress. She had been thinking of the bloodying of the wedding dress as the ultimate calamity of the day.

'Well . . . I'm a bit shaken,' Jane replied. She was tempted to add *'but not stirred'*; but backed away from such flippancy. 'I'll have the dress sent to specialist cleaners. They get quite used to getting blood out of vets' clothes.'

Mrs Ilwand laughed. 'I said not to mind the dress. But what you've got on . . .' She ground to a halt, short of words as her eyes ran up and down Jane's figure, taking in the blatant transparent nature of the replacement dress.

'Shocking, isn't it?'

'Well, it does look more like a nightie. Where did you get it from in a hurry?'

'It *is* a nightie,' Jane explained. 'It was the only all-white thing I could find. Not that anybody will think me entitled to a white wedding when everybody knows that the groom and I have been cohabiting for yonks and if they look too closely they might also notice a slightly bulging waistline . . .'

Mrs Ilwand was still laughing. 'They don't place too much emphasis on that, these days,' she said. 'In the West Highlands things may be different. I was married in that virginial dress but nobody was taken in by—'

'Errr, I'm afraid that's enough girl talk, thank you.' A voice broke in to interrupt the conversation. Jane looked around and realized that a sort of queue had started to form in front of her, at the head of which stood Ian Fellowes, the local detective inspector who was also Deborah's husband and Keith Calder's son-in-law. He was among those who felt obliged to wait before talking to the bride. Now he had lost patience. 'I'm sorry to interrupt so rudely, and Jane, best wishes of course. Now, everybody else please back off. We'll let the full story be known shortly.' Then back to Jane he said in a quieter tone, 'Jane, tell me about this attempted robbery.'

'I can't add anything to what Manfred said,' she replied, now beginning to regret having been so informative about her delay in arriving. She rather wished she had said nothing and explained all later, once she'd actually got married, which was the whole point of why they were all there today, wasn't it?

'You weren't listening to what he said.'

'Yes I was, some of it. And I'm getting married right now. After that I may have time for you. It can't be so very urgent because of the microchip.'

'The what?'

'Didn't Manfred mention it? I stuck the robber with the wrong syringe and put a microchip into him, so you'll have him bang to rights, if that's the proper expression. Until I'm available, go and enjoy yourself. The drinks are on me.'

'And that's you told,' Deborah said to her husband and ushered him away from Jane into the throng of guests, and towards the bar at the other end of the room.

A small stage had been set up at one end of the workshop with a table for the registrar. That lady had put down her glass of champagne and walked to meet Jane and Roland, ready to pounce. 'You're lucky nobody else wants to be born, married or buried this afternoon,' she said. 'So I was able to wait for you.'

'Bless you for that,' Jane said. 'We're just coming.' She realized that she had eaten nothing since breakfast and the big room seemed filled with the smell of a delicious soup that furnished almost the only hot item of food. She did a quick scan of what remained on the buffet. 'God, I'm hungry!' Jane wandered towards the selections on offer, the palm of her hand held up in a stop sign to prevent anyone from coming towards the bride and disturbing her in her primal need to eat before taking the next important step in her life; she certainly wasn't going to look back on this day and only remember the hunger she felt whilst taking her vows.

An electronic keyboard had been borrowed from a choral group based in a local church. At a nod from the registrar the

organist struck up the wedding march and seconds later the
bridal procession was to be seen approaching the improvised
altar with the scantily dressed bride biting into a pork pie.
The Maid of Honour, who was also facing starvation, had
chosen a large slice of quiche. Each had a plastic glass of
champagne in the spare hand. There were multiple flashes
as the members of the photographic section of Kempfield
were busily recording the scene. Instead of the usual respectful
silence accorded to a wedding party approaching the altar
there were handclaps and even a few cheers. Roland and
Manfred had hurried ahead during Jane and Deborah's snack
stop and were already waiting before the registrar's table.
The ladies handed the gentlemen their empty glasses and
wiped their lips on the bridal veil. The groom was noticeably
red in the face. The short ceremony then began.

After the perfunctory ceremony, and the obligatory newly-
married kiss, Jane accepted that she'd have to recount her
earlier experience to the inspector before he forcibly tried
to haul her off to the police station. The manager's office,
just inside the double doors, was made available and Jane,
clinging to her share of the quiche and another large glass
of her own champagne, but with a borrowed sheepskin coat
over the nightdress, found herself recounting her adventure
to Ian Fellowes.

'No, I can't tell you the name of the boy who called me
about the puppy,' she said, 'but I've seen him around
Newton Lauder and I believe his mother's here now, so I
can probably point her out. The puppy was beyond saving
so I put it to sleep to end its suffering. I told the boy how
to hold it but he was overpowered by the thought of death
and he let his grip shift and I got sprayed with blood, that's
where all the time went. I told him to go and get me some
salt – soda would have been better but I didn't want to
waste more time explaining what sort of soda I wanted.
He went to get salt and, next thing I knew, I was being

robbed.' Jane looked as though she was going to end her story there, but she was encouraged to continue by the detective's expectant expression and vigorous note-taking. She felt she had to make more of an effort to be a useful witness, wedding day or not.

'The robber was wearing jeans and what I took to be a T-shirt but it could have been any loose, short-sleeved cotton shirt. He was about my height, quite slim, and he had a woollen mask over his head. I think it was a woollen cap in the local football colours but eyeholes had been cut in it and hemmed with red wool. He had what looked like the help-yourself plastic gloves they have at the garage to protect your hands if you're filling up with diesel. Oh, and it may have been somebody I know, because they used a disguised voice, a sort of rasping whisper.

'He had what looked like the sort of large kitchen knife that you could buy in the ironmonger's shop here. It looked brand new, unused and very sharp. He used the back of the blade to sweep the drugs off my shelves into a carrier bag. Then he told me to open the steel box under the counter, which showed that he already knew about that. After a bit of argy-bargy I told him the combination rather than get my face sliced. And a fat lot of good that will do him,' Jane said, 'because I paid cash into the bank yesterday and he'll have got credit card slips and one or two cheques only. In cash, probably about twenty quid if he's lucky.' Here Jane paused again, but this time not out of a desire to end the conversation, but to gather her thoughts so she could be as accurate as possible about what happened next.

She continued, 'But after I told him the combination of the lock he stooped to look at it and a gap opened between his jeans and his shirt. And I meant to shoot a sleeping draught into him, because I still had half a syringeful handy from putting the puppy to sleep, but what came to my hand was the syringe that puts in microchips. I had already loaded another microchip out of habit because a lot of dogs get restive if they see you fiddling with a syringe. It has a much fatter needle than the usual hypodermic needle and I believe it hurts like hell. Anyway, it hurt him. He gave a high-pitched yelp. I told him that nobody could take the microchip out again or he'd end up on dialysis for the rest of his life, which isn't true but he seemed to believe it. He went out and ran off. And I can give you the number of the microchip. I suppose I should really register him with the Kennel Club,' Jane added reflectively.

Ian Fellowes had been making rapid notes on some typing paper borrowed from the desk. Now he looked at her severely, but apparently he decided that she could be allowed a little latitude on her wedding day. 'Wait here quietly for a couple of minutes,' he said as he quickly slipped out of the room and left Jane to her own thoughts.

Jane felt that she had been engaged in frantic activity for several weeks past, so she was quite happy to relax in the comfortable desk chair and wait for things to happen. Sounds of disco music filtered in; there was laughter and an occasional cheer. It seemed that a good time was being had by all whereas ironically at her own wedding celebration, here she was, on her own in the building manager's office, waiting to be interrogated again. The adrenaline rush wore off and the events of the day so far, as well as the past few days' manic preparation, suddenly caught up with her and she began to fall asleep. She woke with a jump when Ian Fellowes returned, carrying a plate of *hors d'oeuvres* and two large glasses of elderflower champagne. He pushed the door to with his behind and the noise diminished again.

'I was sure you'd still be hungry and thirsty. And obviously you've been very brave.' Ian was suddenly acting like the compassionate friend (as he was in his role of the husband of her Maid of Honour Deborah) rather than a serious police inspector, and Jane, who had not been feeling at all brave, suddenly felt like getting the shakes. 'You said that the voice was disguised,' Ian continued, once again the detective. 'And you said that he was slim and that his yelp was high pitched. Could it have been a woman?'

Jane felt her insides settle down while she had something to puzzle over. She sipped her champagne. This was definitely her best batch ever. Of course, with a larger batch it was easier to keep the temperature constant, she mulled. After a few moments contemplating the merits of the champagne, she caught the detective's questioning and slightly impatient expression and her thoughts returned to the question at hand.

'Possible,' she said. 'Definitely a possibility. I didn't notice it at the time because he or she was flat-chested; but the voice was what in today's jargon they would probably call gender unspecific or unisex or something, rather gruff for a woman's but if it had been above a whisper I think it might have been high-pitched for a man. I didn't see the face or notice the bum. I didn't really see he, she, or whatever walking as they ran off when making their escape, which gives less indication of sex, I always find. In the surgery itself, during the burglary I was concentrating on not getting hurt rather than on my attacker's physique!'

Ian nodded an acceptance of this last comment and while he finished his note-taking there was silence in the office. The music had stopped. Jane could hear a voice and occasional bursts of laughter. The traditional speeches had begun. The programme for a normal wedding had been resumed – without the bride, which Jane thought was really rather odd, but she supposed the planned schedule was being followed religiously and she should be pleased about that considering she'd organized it all in the first place . . .

'Happily nobody was injured,' Ian continued. 'But we can't just let the matter drop because the next attempt might be more determined and the outcome more serious. Now let's talk about drugs. What drugs did he get away with?'

'Not much to interest an addict unless he wanted to cure his kennel cough. Some morphine. I can list the rest when I get the opportunity to check my cupboards and my files,' Jane offered.

'That would be very useful, thanks. Did anything about him suggest that he was an addict?' Ian asked.

Jane put down her plastic champagne glass so that she could shrug more expressively. 'How in God's name would I know?' she enquired rhetorically. 'His head was covered, his eyes were shadowed and there was no other flesh showing except where I stuck in the needle. If it's any help, he – or she – didn't have any twitches or shakes or look particularly sweaty.'

Ian Fellowes refused to take offence. He nodded. 'You haven't given us much to go on. Just a very approximate size. We don't even know what sex. Unless he – or, as you say, she – makes a habit of it, we're up a gum tree. I'll put the word around, we'll put a formal statement on record and hope that it's a one-off, but somehow I doubt it. Go and do your duty dances, Mrs Fox. If you can point out the mother of that boy, do so. And I wish you a long and happy marriage.'

FIVE

The immediate honeymoon of the happy couple took place at home over a period of several hours, the honeymoon proper being planned as a sunshine holiday in Mauritius, some time about the following Christmas if Roland's share of the film advance arrived in time.

The next day being Sunday they would usually have had a 'long lie in'. To a young couple following divergent careers, Sunday morning is usually sacred; but Jane was torn between the needs to do something magical with the borrowed wedding dress, to give Whinmount the cleaning and tidying that had been neglected in the run-up to the wedding day, to restore order to her surgery or to go and help put Kempfield back into some sort of useable state. She was spared the need to choose between all the competing demands by a message from Detective Inspector Ian Fellowes inviting her, in terms not open to refusal, to attend a discussion in his office forthwith. So that decided her and she instead called Helen Maple, the local factotum and sometime cleaner, to spruce up the surgery for the usual fee. That did at least make a token start to her responsibilities.

Roland's introduction to the married state, therefore, consisted of being left alone with a long list of instructions, these to be implemented during the absence of his bride. He set his word processor to boot up and fell asleep in his chair. Honeymoons can be hard work, especially when champagne is involved.

As Jane, dressed in what she thought of as suitably sober garb for a session with the police, drove down the hill and

into the town, she had a view of the streets. The whole
place was emptier than usual and had a slightly hung-over
look about it. Church services would have finished but
perhaps the congregations were lingering in prayer for
forgiveness of any sins that might have been committed at
the wedding party under the influence of elderflower champagne. She parked outside her surgery as usual. Helen's
scooter was already stationed there and she could see a
shadow on the glass as a female figure could be seen
scrubbing up the bloodstains. Jane walked across the
Square to where the old police building frowned reprov-
ingly at the empty spaces. Behind it the tall extension of
the newer building towered more cheerfully.

Newton Lauder had grown into the policing centre for
that part of the Borders but the CID presence was still
small. She entered by the old doorway and was escorted
by DS Bright to Ian's new office on the sunny side of the
new building. Ian was waiting alone. In keeping with the
usual pennywise policy of bureaucracy, his office was not
quite large enough for its purpose. Through his window
she could almost see her home in the distance, peeping
through the trees. Evidently this was to begin as a three-
some discussion. She was offered coffee and although she
had taken breakfast within the previous hour she accepted
gratefully. It turned out to be much better coffee than on
her previous visits, or else she was much thirstier. She
placed a box on a desk that left barely adequate space
around it for three chairs. Bright put a tape recorder beside
it and set it working. Then she had to wait while Ian went
through the routine of recording the date, time, place and
those present. It was a drill that she had encountered previ-
ously when she'd been involved in the search for a missing
boyfriend of her sister's years ago. Back then she'd been
the heroine of the piece, but this time was a different matter.

Ian was looking serious, no longer the jolly wedding
guest. 'There have been no more occurrences involving

knives so far,' he said, 'thanks be, although it's still early days, being only twenty-four hours or so since your burglary. With luck that may be the last of it; but in my experience these incidents often turn out to be the openers for something more serious. The whole of a boozy evening, if you don't mind me referring to your wedding in those terms, went past with remarkably little trouble. Kempfield seems to be more than fulfilling its purpose in keeping the younger and wilder set occupied without recourse to mischief. Of course he – for the sake of simplicity let's go on thinking of the culprit as male – may have decided that crime isn't so easy after all, especially once you're carrying a microchip under your skin; but the first venture into robbery usually happens at a time of desperation. An addict going without, breadwinner losing his job and seeing his family hungry, that sort of thing.' He paused, expecting a comment, but Jane decided to take what he said as a statement of fact requiring no answer. She bowed gravely and waited.

'In case we get a wounding with a sharp blade,' Ian resumed, 'or another knifepoint robbery, I want to be ready to move immediately. I'm asking the uniformed branch to tell all officers to be alert and call in any incidents that might be leading towards knife crime and also to stop and search, very cautiously, anyone of either sex who appears to be carrying a hidden knife or other weapon. Now, let's return to the matter of your statement. Have you thought any more about the person who threatened you? Can you add anything to your description?' Ian asked hopefully.

'No, nothing,' Jane admitted, wondering if her visit to the police station had been in vain. She had been hoping for news of a possible arrest at the very least.

'Did you perhaps notice any aroma that might give us a clue? Perfume? Aftershave? Unpleasant body odour?'

'Nothing that I can recall. I only had the intruder's company for barely a couple of minutes, remember, during which I was a trifle overwrought.'

'Yes, of course. Now, we haven't yet identified the youth who brought you the puppy. Have you been able to identify his mother yet? Do you think that this boy could possibly have gone outside, donned the mask and returned?'

'Not in the time available,' Jane said. 'Quite impossible. Anyway, he went ahead and pushed a packet of salt through the letter box and I really can't see an attacker doing that. Or might he see not doing so as perhaps looking suspicious? Anyway, I was being attacked at the time he pushed the salt through the letter box, so it couldn't have been him. And I'm afraid I haven't been able to match up mother and son yet, so I can't help you with his identification. But as I don't think it could be him, perhaps there's no point in worrying about that?' Jane asked hopefully, dreading a long drawn out process of needless identifying of someone who wasn't going to help lead them anywhere anyway.

'It could be possible that they were in it together, using the puppy as a distraction to get you on your own in your surgery perhaps.' Ian again looked rather hopeful at this possibility, but moved on to his next question as he saw Jane's frown and shake of the head. 'OK, well, if we get our hands on your assailant, would he have your DNA or the puppy's on him?'

Jane almost laughed. 'Not a hope! I never touched him except with a fat hypodermic needle. He might have got a little of the puppy's blood on him, I suppose. Speaking of the puppy, can I have the body incinerated yet?'

Ian looked at her sharply and then shook his head. 'Not yet. It'll prove to be a huge waste of expensive time but I'd better have the Forensics Department in Edinburgh look it over. Now tell me all about microchips.'

'I don't know a lot about microchips,' Jane admitted. 'Just enough to implant one – I use a simple syringe although you can get more sophisticated gadgets – and to read the number of the bar code off the reader. We then register that number and if the patient turns up, alive or dead, we can find out who was the owner at the time. I've never known anybody want it taken out again; if there's a change of ownership we only have to notify the registering office, but in this case the bandit might well want to be rid of it. If the chip was just under the skin that would be easy, but in my aggravation I jabbed it well in. I suggest that you have all doctors and surgeons warned to report if they're approached to remove a chip.'

'Good point. We'll do that. Bright.' Ian looked over at DS Bright and nodded in acknowledgement that this was to be his job. 'But, Jane, could *you* remove that chip from his back?' he continued.

'Yes, I suppose I could. I put it in so I'd know roughly where to look for it. I could remove it from the same general area of a sheep or a horse so, given a patient who would accept an anaesthetic, I could take it out of a person. I would be breaking the law but I could do it.'

'Then we'd better include all vets in the circular. Who else?'

The two men watched Jane hopefully while she thought about it. She felt as if they were waiting for her to sing or to do a conjuring trick. 'Dentists, probably. ER nursing staff perhaps. If I think of any other profession, I'll tell you.'

'Do that. And we'll try to keep an eye on you for your safety, though I suppose you'll be the last person he'd allow near him carrying something sharp. How close would you have to get to tell whether an animal had been microchipped?'

'Really close. It's not as though I landed him with the sort of transponder they attach to wildlife. This is only designed to give a number close up. I don't begin to get a reading until I'm almost touching the animal. If you were thinking of a scanner that could pick up the presence of a microchipped person in a crowd . . .?'

'I was.'

'Standard equipment wouldn't do it. I brought my reader along to show you.' She opened the plastic box she'd brought with her and put on Ian's desk and drew out a neat instrument resembling an early mobile phone. 'You should go and talk to Mr Ilwand at the TV and computer shop. He designs that sort of gear. I seem to remember that there was a gadget on the market some years ago for detecting microwaves if they were escaping from a micro-wave oven and endangering the cook. It had to be taken off the market because it was too sensitive. He might be able to cobble together something like that for you—'

Jane was interrupted by a knock and the entry of a young man in plain clothes and plastic gloves. He had once brought her a shorthaired pointer puppy for neutering. He turned out to be one of Ian's constables. He delivered a paper bag to Ian, gave Jane a friendly nod and departed.

'This,' Ian said, 'will be a selection from the rubbish swept up and emptied from the waste bins at Kempfield last night. We were lacking any starting point whatever. It seemed to me that our culprit either did or did not visit Kempfield in an attempt to establish some sort of alibi. If not, then we start with the comparatively limited number of people of suitable physique who were not present. But you said that he had stuffed a handful of your duplicates into his pockets and he would have had to get rid of them. I really couldn't see him having a little private bonfire. And as long as he was walking around with his pockets full of your credit card slips he was marked. So I had my boys bag up the rubbish collected from Kempfield, separating out and discarding obvious irrelevancies like toffee papers. A couple of beat bobbies are looking in the town's waste bins. Give me a moment for a glance at this little lot . . .'

From his desk drawer he took similar gloves to those the constable had been wearing and drew them on. He sniffed the bag suspiciously and then tipped it out on to his unused blotter. 'It's a long shot. I don't suppose there will be anything,' he began, 'but when you start with nothing—' His voice broke off abruptly. There were more paper scraps than Jane would have expected. Ian took a ballpoint pen from his pocket and turned over two of them. 'Credit card slips!' he said. 'No, don't touch them, they won't have been finger-printed yet, but take a look and tell me if you issued them.'

Jane was experienced enough in the ways of the police to know that her evidence might later become important. 'I identify these two slips as having been printed by the credit card machine in my office,' she said carefully. 'I remember putting through both transactions. You jammy devil! But how stupid to dump that at Kempfield!'

Ian shrugged. 'Not necessarily. He kept the money that he was after but he didn't want to be caught with anything on him as incriminating as the credit card slips so he got rid of them in the first litter bins that he came to – prob-ably before getting rid of his gloves unless he really is stupid.' He shuffled the papers back into the bag. 'This can go for examination and fingerprinting. So . . . it would seem that our knife-wielding robber came straight to Kempfield. Bright, go next door, get on the phone and invite Lucas Fraine to join me immediately. We'll see if Mr Fraine can possibly say who arrived at Kempfield and joined the wedding party just before the bride made her spectacular entry or soon afterwards. I'm sorry,' he added quickly, 'I shouldn't pull your leg about your state of dress. You looked quite—'

He was interrupted, rather to Jane's relief, by the ringing of one of the two phones on Ian's desk. He snatched it up. 'I thought I said no interruptions.'

The female voice was quite unflustered. 'Yes, I know, unless there were reports of a potential knife crime, you said,' the voice insisted. 'Then you'd want to know and that's what I've got here.'

'I'll take the call,' Ian said.

'I'm just putting it through,' said the voice complacently. Ian would not have been given the option of refusing it.

Ian listened, his brow growing ever angrier, to several minutes of a report in a voice so thickly accented that such words as escaped in Jane's direction were unintelligible. He grunted an acknowledgement and said, 'Tell them to bring the boy in. And have the place locked up until we know what we're looking for.' He hung up.

'They got him?' Jane said.

'No such luck! Just what I was afraid of has happened – a knifepoint robbery. You know Hugh Dodd?'

'Yes. He cuts my grass for me once a week in summer. But it couldn't be him, he's more thickset than my robber and a little taller.'

Ian frowned at her leap to an erroneous conclusion. 'Nobody's suggesting that he's the guilty party. He was on duty at the filling station, taking petrol money. Somebody with a knife walked in and emptied the till. He isn't hurt.'

SIX

DI Fellowes was looking at Jane thoughtfully. She was quite used to being looked at by men but she was now a respectably married lady and if he was relishing the erotic memory of her in her nightdress and bridal veil, which must surely have resembled something out of a soft porn film, then that, she thought, was quite enough of that. 'You've finished with me?' she asked.

Ian snapped out of his reverie. 'That's exactly what I was wondering. On the whole, because you seem to be a kingpin – or queenpin – of whatever's going on, I'll ask you to remain for the moment. You and young Dodd may help to refresh each other's memories. And you sometimes come up with helpful ideas.'

Jane switched her attention back to the identity of the robber. 'Well here's another one,' she said. 'At least I hope you'll find it helpful.'

'I'm sure I will, but keep it on ice for a few minutes. Bright, get hold of Morrison. I want him to collect all the usual samples from the vet's surgery and from the filling station's office and shop, immediately. Make it clear that this is no longer his day off.' Morrison, Jane knew, was one of Ian's two constables, the one with training as a SOCO. 'Now, Jane.'

Jane handed over the surgery key and pulled herself together. 'Eh?' she said.

'Your bright idea.'

'Oh yes. First, I'd better say that I'm sorry. I told Helen Maple to clean my surgery.'

Ian did not say a rude word but Jane was in little doubt that he was thinking it from the way his frown deepened and his shoulders slumped in resignation that another aspect of this investigation was going to prove fruitless.

Jane said quickly, 'It would seem that your wildest guess has come off. The guilty party hurried up to Kempfield, presumably in case he might have been missed if he'd failed to show up. Because GG was one of the leading spirits of the Creative Adventure Centre and because he was first and foremost a photographer, we have a thriving photography section and, perhaps because I was presenting a certain sort of picture . . .' She felt her face burning at the thought of so many images of her with her more intimate parts visible through diaphanous lace and found it hard to continue.

'It's all right,' Ian said. 'I understand.'

'Well, the cameras were hard at work during the wedding. You could have read a newspaper by the flashes as Deborah and I walked up what I suppose we have to think of as the aisle. The darkrooms at Kempfield will be busy for the next few days or weeks, being tidied up and put back the way they belong. When you see Lucas Fraine you could suggest that he gets the photography members to print off every shot of people, along with the time of the photograph if the camera is so equipped. You could get everybody who was there to name anyone within a certain age bracket . . .'

Ian smiled on her and this time she was sure that it was not just that he was recalling her in her nightdress. 'Yes,' he said, 'I do find it helpful. But who pays for the huge volume of printing paper is something we'll have to think about. That stuff comes expensive.'

'Cheapskate! It's grossly overpriced but most of them are using digital cameras now and you can make a perfectly good print from them on typing paper. Not exhibition quality but good enough to recognize a wedding guest.'

Ian had the grace to look ashamed. 'I should have thought of that, but I leave that sort of thing to the boys who are trained for it. We'll put it in hand, starting with the digital users. Do me another favour. Sit quietly for a minute while I prepare a short email to Edinburgh to let my chiefs know what's afoot.'

It was a fine day. Two fine days in succession made an occasion worthy of a memorial in bronze. Jane looked out at the sunshine smiling on the town while Ian typed away at almost professional speed. They were both interrupted by the return of DS Bright accompanied by a snub-nosed, vacant-faced youth. This was Hugh Dodd, a casual worker at Ledbetter's garage and generally supposed to be a by-blow of the elder Ledbetter. Ledbetter himself made a third.

'Here!' Ledbetter Senior said. 'I don't know how much cash the man with the knife got hold of but there's no need to ruin my business for the rest of my day. And what about all the drivers who'll be getting stuck at the roadside?'

'Your office and shop stay closed until we've examined them,' Ian said firmly. 'Petrol sales can continue. Sit somebody out at the pumps with a card table and a cash box to take the money.'

'I need young Hugh. That's his job,' Ledbetter Senior demanded.

'You can't have him. Do it yourself,' was the detective's retort.

Ian was obviously not going to be overawed by a local businessman. Ledbetter tried a more conciliatory tone. 'But the read-out of the amounts due is inside the shop. And so's the credit card machine.'

Ian had his own worries. 'Then I can see you have a problem or two. Go away and solve them.'

Ledbetter, waving his arms, made a grumbling departure escorted by DS Bright. Ian called to his departing back, 'The bank's hole-in-the-wall is only a minute's walk away. They can draw cash.' The comment was not acknowledged. Ian glared at the youth. 'You were robbed at knifepoint. Yes?'

'It weren't my bloody fault,' the boy whined.

'Nobody said it was but you make me wonder. Now shut up for a minute.' There was silence while Ian added a paragraph to his email and hit a key that Jane assumed would send it. With his superiors in Edinburgh alerted he returned his attention to Hugh Dodd. 'Now calm down and tell me exactly what happened.'

DS Bright had returned. He set the recorder to work again. Dodd avoided looking directly at it. 'We don't open 'til ten on a Sunday morning,' he said. 'I opened up and started taking the money. You usually get een or twa drivers early who've been waiting half the nicht. After that it goes quiet. Mr Ledbetter had emptied the till yestreen, except for a float for making change. You get the odd sale of a gallon or twa, mostly two-stroke, so you need change.'

'What time did he empty the till?' Ian asked.

Dodd opened his mouth, closed it again and smacked himself on his forehead. ''Twasn't yestreen, it were the day before. Bank doesn't open on Saturday and the boss doesn't like the night safe; he's had disagreeances with the bank staff afore noo. Friday it were, just afore it closed. Yestreen was busy, I could tell when I opened up, but mostly not in coins. In notes I'd say about twa hunner.'

Ian nodded. Two hundred pounds in notes would be a reasonable guess, with credit cards in such general use for the purchase of petrol and diesel. 'Now tell me exactly what happened.'

Young Dodd closed his eyes in thought for a few seconds. 'I'd just taken twenty quid on Mastercard from Quent Williamson for that Morgan of his and he'd driven off. And old Mr Mowatt had just filled his can with lead-free for his mower and two-stroke for his strimmer. He paid in cash. I gave him change and a receipt and he'd just walked out the door when this chiel walks in – must've been waiting outside to catch me alone. He had his toorey bonnet pulled down over his gizz and holes cut for his een.' Ian opened his mouth but Dodd answered his question before it could be asked. 'In fitba colours it was. He had a bloody great knife, just like the one my mam chops up the veggies with, and he jouked under the flap and came behind the counter, which isna' allowed, and next I knew his knife was at my throat. He told me to open the till. So I opened the bloody till. Whit else would I dae?'

'I'd have done the same,' Ian reassured him. 'Tell me about his voice.'

'Hoarse. Sort of whispery.'

'Man or woman?'

'It was a bloke for sure. Quinies don't hold up filling stations with knives.'

'But from the voice alone could you be sure that it was a man?'

Again Dodd paused for thought. (Ian was patient. He said sometimes that he preferred a witness who took time to think about what he was going to say to one who blurted out a quick reply and was then too stubborn to amend it.) 'Not just from the voice, but a man has a different shape to his chest and bum and walks different.' Dodd got up from his chair. 'See, a woman walks like this . . .' Showing a rare talent for mime, Dodd walked around what vacant floor space the room had. He had the tilt of the hips and the placing of the feet to perfection. Jane decided to monitor her own walk and prevent her bottom from swaying so much.

'So you're sure that it was a man?' Ian said. 'Or a skilled actress?'

Dodd resumed his seat. 'How d'you mean?'

'Could it have been a woman who could walk like a man just as cleverly as you can imitate a woman's walk?'

It was the right tack. Dodd flushed with pleasure at the compliment to his acting ability but it still got them no further. 'Don't know, do I?'

'Think about it and tell me if and when you make up your mind. What sort of size and build?'

'About my height but a bit skinnier.'

'And how was he dressed?'

'Jeans. Plain white T-shirt, no printing on it. It was spotted with something but not a colour. The spots looked grey-like. Could've been paint or some kind of dirt. Oil, maybe. White trainers, new-looking. Digital Timex watch with expanding bracelet, all chrome. Sorry, best I can do.'

'You've done very well,' Ian said. 'Better than Miss Highsmith. Mrs Fox, I should say.'

'Hang on, I'm not finished,' Dodd added, now confident and on a roll. 'There was a smell but I dunno what of.'

Ian switched his eyes to Jane. 'Well?'

'I didn't notice any odour. I told you so.'

Young Mr Dodd grinned suddenly, showing two gaps where teeth should have been. 'Hey! He done you too?'

'I'm afraid so. He didn't get much money,' Jane said. 'I was wondering, though. Were his hands roughened by hard work? Or soft? Were they stained at all?'

'Didn't look at his hands.'

'Nor did I. He had gloves on with me. Maybe with you too? Could you make a guess as to what shape of head he had?' Dodd looked baffled. 'Listen,' Jane said. 'Some people have a round sort of head like a football. Some have a pointy sort of head, not very wide but . . .' Jane came to a halt while she tried to conjure up the right words.

'Streamlined like?'

It came to Jane that a boy like Dodd, with a definite interest in motorbikes, might well see heads in that strange way. 'Yes, just like that.'

'No, he wasn't like that. More sort of up-and-down.'

Jane managed to extract a meaning from the words. 'Like a chimney-pot or a top hat, you mean? High but not going back much at the back and with not too big a nose? Like the minister at the Old Kirk?'

'Don't say any more just now,' Ian interrupted them. 'We don't want to put ideas into his head. What did you think, yourself?' Ian looked pointedly at Jane, his expression expectant.

'I wasn't looking at his head, I was watching the knife and wondering if I dared give him a shot of anaesthetic. And then I went and grabbed the wrong syringe.'

'I'll gather up some officers of around the right size and borrow some bonnets and we'll have a parade of head shapes. Thank you both very . . .' Ian paused and raised his eyebrows at the screen of his laptop. 'I've got an answer already. That's quick. Phenomenal. You can both go now, but I'll want you again. Stay in touch.'

Jane walked out with young Dodd for company. 'What was that about a syringe?' he asked.

'I stuck the mannie with a microchip,' Jane said, 'but don't you go telling everybody about it. Mr Fellowes wouldn't want that.'

Just as Jane was about to walk out the main door of the police station, with Dodd in tow, she was called back by a shout from down the corridor. 'Jane, sorry Mrs Fox . . . can I have a quick word?' Fellowes was striding up the corridor, suit tails flapping, as he rushed to catch Jane before she left. 'I'm sorry, can I just steal you for a few minutes more? It's very important,' Ian implored her.

'Oh,yes, I suppose so, it's only my honeymoon for God's sake!' Jane felt she had to make Ian feel slightly guilty for demanding her presence once again on this day after her wedding. But truthfully she knew if she wasn't here at the station that she'd be doing some other chore, which would probably involve a lot more physical effort, so she was perfectly happy to put her brain to some good use in helping the investigation along.

'That's much appreciated, thank you.' Ian showed his appreciation and lead her back down the corridor and through a plain door labelled 'Interview Room 1'.

Inside was sitting DS Bright and another man, this one probably in his mid to late sixties, with a weather-beaten complexion and the brown leathery skin that comes with working outside most of your adult life. He also had the large and work-hardened hands to go with the impression that Jane had of him so far as a manual worker of some sort.

'This is Mr Mowatt. He is also a witness in this investigation and I'd like to conduct a joint interview with the two of you now, in the hope that you can remind each other of any significant details.' Fellowes introduced the man to Jane and gestured to her to sit down on the other side of the table from the older man and DS Bright. After going through the legal procedure for recording an interview, Detective Fellowes was ready to begin the next round of questions.

'Mr Mowatt, why were you at Ledbetter's garage earlier today?' Fellowes began.

'Well, I needed to get some petrol, didn't I, for my Monday job up at Hay Lodge. There's strimming and mowing of the lawns that's got to be done early, so I was getting prepared and I hates filling up on a Sunday afternoon with all the commuters – they get on my nerves.'

'OK, Mr Mowatt, thank you. And what did you see as you were leaving the garage shop?'

'Well, I was just coming out the door of the shop when a person came out of nowhere and sneaked in through the door behind me. It was odd because the person had a hat pulled down very low over their head, so I couldn't see their face at all, and they were all hunched over like as if they didn't want to be recognized, which I thought was also a bit strange. It got me thinking as I was walking over to my car, so I turned round, but by then the person was almost inside the shop and all I could see was a plaster on the back of his neck. I then just thought I was being silly to suspect anything and anyway I wanted to get home in time for the beginning of the racing on TV, so I thought no more about it until you called me to say there'd been a robbery and had I noticed anything strange. Well, that's about the gist of it. Hope I've been helpful,' Mr Mowatt added.

'You have, thank you, sir.' DS Bright answered on behalf of Inspector Fellowes who wasn't reacting and seemed instead to be in the process of mulling things over in his mind. 'Any memory of what the person was wearing at all, sir?' DS Bright took the opportunity to get in some questions of his own.

'Hmmm, well, jeans, like everyone does nowadays, and a white top. Oh, and old scruffy-looking trainers. I always looks at a person's shoes. That's what got me wondering about him, really. The shoes looked uncared for – made him look untrustworthy.' Mr Mowatt was pleased with this supposition of his and waited for Ian to jump on this nugget of information. But Detective Fellowes was still engrossed in thought, so Mr Mowatt sat back disappointed and had to wait.

A minute of silence later and Ian was ready to ask his next question. 'And how do you think the culprit arrived at the petrol station, Mr Mowatt? Did you see any type of vehicle that didn't seem to belong to other people filling up?'

'Well, there was no one else there as I left, mine was the only car in the forecourt, but I did notice a bicycle propped up against the wall, very new-looking it was too, so it could have been his, but I never saw him arrive or leave so I wouldn't like to say.'

'OK, that's very useful, Mr Mowatt.' Fellowes thanked him and then turned to Jane, who up until this point had been wondering why she had been involved in proceedings so far. 'Jane, sorry Mrs Fox, can you confirm any of the details that Mr Mowatt has brought to our attention? Did you see a plaster on your attacker's neck? Or a new bicycle outside your surgery?' Ian asked hopefully.

'No, I'm afraid not. I definitely didn't notice a plaster

on his neck. I suppose I never really saw my attacker from the back – only once he was leaving and by then I was so glad to see him go that I crumpled down to the floor in relief. So no, sorry. And I never noticed any bicycle. As I said to you, I heard him running off and it was definitely feet on gravel I heard, not tyres.'

'OK, fair enough.' Ian looked disappointed again, annoyed that he was once more no further along in their investigation despite there being all these new witnesses. 'You may both go – for real this time,' Fellowes added and smiled a thank you to Jane.

She made her escape quickly this time, preparing herself not to turn round if she heard her name being shouted down the corridor again.

SEVEN

J ane arrived home hungry. Roland, who had lived a bach-
elor life for several years before meeting Jane, was
pottering vaguely in the kitchen. He was perfectly
capable of catering for himself but preferred to mime
helplessness on the grounds that nothing was where he
had put it and he had no idea what victuals they had in
stock.

Jane sighed. First she phoned her own surgery answering
machine but there had been no emergency calls. She still
felt hard done by. She, after all, was pursuing a profession
with obligations and long but fairly regular hours while
her old partner but new husband was engaged in an elastic
operation much of which – the cerebral part – could be
pursued while carrying out some unconnected manual task.
Washing up and bed-making sprang first to mind but any
suggestion that he should take over such responsibilities
while composing mentally his next few pages would
usually bring on a well-reasoned and beautifully worded
riposte to the effect that such divided interest was unwork-
able. Jane had admitted defeat and given up trying to
encourage such domestic help from him on the under-
standing that any 'manly' tasks that wanted doing were
very much his domain. So far he had yet to be tested on
that score.

Roland was looking out of the kitchen window at the
sodden world outside when the phone rang. He'd barely
answered it with the words 'the Fox residence', when the
caller obviously demanded to speak with Jane as quickly
as possible and Roland obligingly obeyed.

Jane listened attentively, saying very little and wandered

about the kitchen getting various bits and pieces out of pantry cupboards and fridges. At last the call was over.

'What was all the kerfuffle about?' he asked. 'Still your visitor with the cutlass?'

Jane had managed to begin assembling some semblance of a meal whilst on the phone, mostly composed of what had been surplus to requirements for the wedding feast. 'Well,' Jane replied and readied herself to fill in Roland on all the details of her earlier meeting with the detective and her subsequent recent phone call, as that was who had just demanded her attention for the last ten minutes or so. 'Fellowes asked me in earlier as the same bloke has now committed a new offence. He visited the filling station office this morning and emptied the till. Gave Hugh Dodd a hell of a fright. He got away with a lot more cash than he did from my place so maybe we'll get a little peace and quiet until he's spent it.'

'Not if he's being blackmailed or if it was the down payment on a luxury car. Let me know if he gets arrested. I'd like a word with him. There must be a lot of valuable material going to waste.'

'Writers!' Jane said. 'You never shut down. Anyway, some new bits are being added to the equation, it seems. After I sat in on the interview with Hugh Dodd earlier this afternoon, Fellowes then asked me to stay on whilst he had a chat with old Mr Mowatt, who was a witness as well as he'd just finished paying for some petrol he needed for his mower just as the burglar arrived at the petrol station. Anyway, it transpires that the attacker had a plaster on the back of his neck as if covering a pluke, as he calls it – you know, a rather unpleasant spot. So keep your eyes open. Ian's asked me to mention it to you.

'And he's asked me to check with you that whilst you were waiting anxiously for my arrival at our wedding, did you notice anybody who came in at just about the same time, somebody young, probably male, probably on a motorbike or scooter, possibly by pushbike. If pushbike, it may have been very clean and polished. Or new,' she added. This may have been the new information supplied by Mr Mowatt's witness statement, but as Jane realized, the burglar's gain from the robbery at her surgery would not have covered a new bicycle, so it was unlikely to be significant.

'Not off the top of the head but I'll ask Manfred.'

'I suppose there wasn't any of my champagne left.' Jane's thoughts had now moved on and she felt she surely deserved something more exciting than water with her dinner tonight.

'Funny you should say that! There was about enough to fill a bathtub that they didn't manage to finish so I decanted some into a few cider screw-tops and brought it home. The rest seems to have vanished into the private stocks of members. Do you want a glass?'

'Do I ever! But first I must go and see what I can do about that wedding dress. Roley, did you mind that I had to make rather an indecent picture of myself?'

'I thought you looked quite gorgeous,' Roland said.

'That's not quite answering the same question,' Jane said, but it was as far as Roland would commit himself.

Ian Fellowes arrived home rather late that evening, but he had phoned to warn Deborah. His meal was waiting for him, still warm though slightly desiccated. He had already told her about the second knifepoint robbery.

'I had to make sure that everything was set for tomorrow, including getting Lucas Fraine to list everybody who was present at Jane's whoopdedoo. They're supposed to be sending me a coachload of woodentops. Bright's prepared to bet that we only get two to interview the whole lot of them and he's probably right.'

'You've got to get out of the habit of referring to the uniformed branch as woodentops,' Deborah said severely.

'You know they hate it.' Deborah paused, her mind having turned to more important questions. 'I wonder how Jane makes that elderflower champagne. I'd like to find out while elderflowers are still in season. Mine never comes out quite so . . . What would you call it?'

'Mind-numbing,' Ian said after a moment's thought. Then his train of thought moved back to the matter at hand. 'You arrived with Jane. It seems that the robber must have headed straight up the hill to Kempfield. Who did you see arrive at about the same time? And did you overtake a cyclist on the hill?'

'I don't remember anybody but I'll think about it.'

'Do that. And add this to the equation. Jane asked an interesting question about head shapes. Since then, I've been looking at heads through new eyes and she was right. There is a usual shape of head but only about a third of the Caucasian part of the human race conforms to it. The others may be sort of sharp-faced – Dodd called it stream-lined – or round like a ball, with or without sticking-out ears. But he described his visitor as having a head like a chimney-pot, more or less cylindrical but with protruding ears. See if that image doesn't jog your memory.'

'I'll try,' Deborah said doubtfully. 'But the only one I remember won't help you much.'

'Try me anyway.'

'All right. But I only noticed because it was a car very like yours and there was a pair of gloves above the dash-board with one finger sticking up rather rudely so that an oncoming driver thought that he was getting the finger and shook his fist in reply. Elspeth Bryden was driving it – Elspeth Stevenson she used to be but she married Angus Bryden. They were both at school with me. I liked her a lot but I couldn't stand him. Great tall streak of nothing very much; I wouldn't trust him near the baby's piggy-bank. She overtook the limo on the climb up to Kempfield. I was going to speak to you later about overtaking when you couldn't see far enough ahead, but when we got out of the limo I saw that Elspeth was driving and it wasn't you at all. She said to me later that she'd been held up by her mother-in-law on the phone wanting to know where Angus had got to. Well, almost everyone else knew where he'd got to – what the Americans call *first base* with that gipsy-looking girl who serves in the Canal Bar, but his mother would never believe that he was anything but a perfect gentleman. That was the fat woman who talked loudly while you were trying to make your speech.'

'Tell me again in the morning,' Ian said. 'I'm not really taking in the rush of information just now, between being tired and trying to think ahead to all that I'll have to do in the morning.'

'I'll leave you in peace, then. But first let me just mention that there were two or three motor scooters and there was already a row of about ten pushbikes in the racks at the side of the car park.'

'Was any of them remarkably clean and shiny?' asked Fellowes, in reference to Mr Mowatt's description of the witness possibly arriving at the petrol station on such a vehicle.

'Not that I noticed. In fact, several of them and the motor scooters all looked due to go in the nearest skip. But at least for most people it would be downhill all the way home.'

Ian sat up and frowned. 'Did you notice whether any of the pushbikes had a saddlebag?' he asked.

Deborah matched his frown. 'Not to say notice, but I think several of them did. Why?'

'Because he arrived at two different scenes-of-crime carrying a largish knife. He might have dangled it down a trouser-leg though I wouldn't have fancied that much myself. Some clumsy beggar would only have to knock into you . . . Anyway, it doesn't seem the premeditated sort of crime for which somebody might have made a special sheath and he wouldn't want to walk around carrying it openly and he certainly didn't drive to the door of Ledbetter's garage, he very likely cycled there. He was wearing a T-shirt as well, so even less places to hide a knife.'

'But he could have carried a kitchen-type knife loose in a saddlebag,' Deborah said. 'I'm with you now. You don't see many handlebar baskets these days so a saddlebag does seem likely. I'll keep my eyes open for a bright-looking pushbike with a saddlebag.'

'You do that,' said her husband, pouring himself a large glass of elderflower champagne.

EIGHT

Monday morning came in wet and Mondayish. Ian Fellowes made a point of being early to work. He had beaten his own staff to it and there was no sign of the promised help, not even an email. That was all he needed to start the week as it would probably go on. However, he was slightly mollified to see that the former gymnasium, now available for functions or for use as an incident room, had been equipped with desks, chairs, phones, a computer and all the other paraphernalia of the HQ for a complex case – presumably for *his* complex case, though as things were going he would not have been surprised to find that the room had been annexed for use in connection with a missing tomcat.

DS Bright arrived seconds behind him and reassured him on the latter point. Ian's two bright young DCs followed almost immediately. Emails being conspicuous by their absence, Ian sent the younger DC, Hopgood by name, to collect Lucas Fraine's list from him, failing which Fraine was to be fetched in to explain himself. Ian began to feel better, but only until a liveried Vauxhall arrived bringing the promised collator and three borrowed DCs with no promises of further help.

If Hugh Dodd had been obliging enough to throw himself on the point of the knife like some Roman warrior falling on his sword, Ian mused, the town would have been clogged with personnel: officers for fingertip searches, scene of crime specialists, collators and others who always seemed ready to browse around a death scene without ever quite admitting who the hell they were. (Ian was hard pressed to remember many of the finer details because in the event of a death by foul play a more senior officer than a mere DI would undoubtedly take charge, hogging the credit but not any blame that happened to be going, and only the best and most senior would ever pause to explain anything.)

With Ian's other DC, Morrison (the only one to have received any training as a SOCO) being sent to examine and release the two crime scenes, aided by a borrowed beat bobby, it was a small team that assembled at the desks in front of the whiteboards that had been recovered from the store and hooked up on the long wall facing the door. If the next victim of the knifeman (and Ian was sure that they had not seen the last victim) should lose blood, the numbers would increase exponentially and more so if that unfortunate should happen to . . . Ian was suddenly amazed to realize the incredible number of euphemisms there were for *dying* and *death*. Before Ian had time to dwell much further on the matter, the return of DC Hopgood with Mr Fraine's list of names increased the team considerably.

Bright, who was used to Ian's *modus operandi*, stood at the whiteboard while Ian explained what had happened so far. Ian detested slang such as 'Chummy', so it was under the heading 'The Knifeman' that the first list began to extend:

> Jeans. Plain white T-shirt, no printing on it, spotted with something but not a colour.
> The spots looked grey. Could've been paint or some kind of dirt or oil.
> Dark hair. White trainers, new-looking. (Old Mowatt says old or dirty.)
> Digital Timex watch with expanding bracelet, all chrome. (Hugh Dodd)
> Rasping, whispery voice, probably assumed. Upright head. Protruding ears. Plaster on back of neck.
> Bike clean and shining. Possibly saddlebag.

Probably but not necessarily male.
Microchipped.

Bright sat down beside the whiteboard but Ian stayed on his feet as he addressed the room. 'The reason is simple as to why the possibility of Knifeman being Knifewoman is not dismissed. I don't always trust the advice given by psychologists but in this instance I phoned our usual shrink. He said that there is a slight statistical bias towards females when stabbings are concerned. He went into some unpleasant details about women, envy and penetration, which you can look up in the textbooks for yourselves. Just take it that the possibility of a female Knifeman exists.

'If I sent you into the town to bring back anybody fitting this description – ignoring the plaster that may have been intended to mislead us, and anyway is easy to remove – I doubt if this room would hold them and we don't at the moment have any fingerprints or DNA samples for elimination purposes.

'The one certain means of identification is that Miss Highsmith, as she was then – she's Mrs Fox now – managed to stab him with a microchip during the robbery. I say *managed* but in fact she intended to put him to sleep but the wrong syringe came to hand.' At this point – with a sweep of his hand – Ian acknowledged Jane, who had just entered through the door at the back of the room – having been summoned earlier with a phone call.

Jane coughed, more to gain attention than to clear her throat, and said, 'Let me break in at this point and save you some time. I did some research yesterday. I tested a microchip and repeated my test with the microchip taped on to my husband's back. The result was surprising, but Knifeman would have no difficulty discovering the same facts. Incidentally, I was horrified to find that the apron the manufacturers gave me as protection when I bought the device is not very effective, probably because it has to be flexible, necessitating small gaps. Thankfully in my condition –' Jane laid an instinctive hand on her belly – 'I have hardly taken any X-rays recently. So in terms of blocking out the microchip so that the reader couldn't pick up on it, I discovered that lead foil is not very good and is very fragile. It tears easily. But aluminium foil worked very well at first and, being cheap and common, could be replaced quickly and easily. And, of course, being very thin, it would be difficult to detect by feel under clothing. On the other hand crumpling soon ruined its effectiveness. Make what you like of that. In future, I shall take X-rays with my lead apron backed by kitchen foil. May I leave now?' Jane had said her piece and was ready to go and actually earn a living.

'Many thanks for your contribution,' Ian said to her retreating back as Jane slipped out of the room. Ian Fellowes took a few seconds to absorb the information. 'We shall have to devise a new drill for testing suspects,' he said. 'Meanwhile, continue doing it the simple way. So far we have managed to borrow two microchip readers, but Morrison's next task is to phone vets and anybody else anyone can think of in the hope of borrowing one or two more. Don't forget that you have to hold it close to the suspect's left kidney to get a signal, use any excuse to crumple any foil under the clothing and don't be concerned if the device tells you that the suspect is a Pomeranian terrier or a pat of butter. Any signal at all will do.'

When the laughter had subsided, Ian went on, 'By my reckoning that leaves us three DCs plus myself and my sergeant with two microchip readers to interrogate the six people listed by Lucas Fraine, the manager of Kempfield, as having arrived at about the same time as the bridal party. Don't forget to ask each of them who they remember seeing arrive around the same time – with quite a large margin either side, because it took Mrs Fox some time to change and clean up the puppy's blood and, conversely, we don't know how long it took the knifeman to get up the hill. He may even have gone home to stick another plaster over the puncture, because a microchip is inserted through a fairly fat needle compared to the hypodermics you may be remembering. Incidentally, you'd also have thought that there'll be some broken skin or early scarring where the microchip went in – at least for the next few days – so any excuse to actually take a look at the person's flesh would be very useful. But be tactful about this for obvious reasons.' Again there was the sound of light laughter around the room.

Ian continued, 'It would have been very helpful if some of the stolen money had been in unusual denominations, but no such luck! If it seems appropriate and without raising a storm it might be helpful to know which of our young people has started spending money or settling a debt.

'Any questions?' There were none. 'Any suggestions as to what I may not have thought of yet?' Again a deathly hush. 'Pass any possibly relevant information or ideas as it's obtained to the collator, Mr . . .?'

'Nicholson,' said the collator. He was in his sixties, bald and stooped, but his eyes were very sharp.

'Mr Nicholson. He will have a radio, but in case that's busy take the phone number with you and leave a message on the answering machine that I see somebody – DS Bright? – has thoughtfully obtained for us. Follow up any leads but check with Mr Nicholson before following up a line of your own in case somebody else is already sniffing along that trail.

'Same time and place tomorrow morning. And dress down a bit. You all look too policemanlike for the generally young people you'll be mixing with. That's all. Go and get on with it. Settle between yourselves who goes where.'

Several chairs scraped and there was a snapping shut of notebooks. Ian was left with Mr Nicholson. 'How did I do?' he asked.

Nicholson had been tidying up some of Bright's script on the whiteboard. He faced round. 'You did well, sir,' he said. 'I think they were all pleased to be informed and considered. Makes a change.'

Ian's attention was caught by the wording. 'You're ex-CID?'

'Did my time with the Met. Retired as a DI. Retirement was boring and the pension ungenerous so I applied for work as a civilian collator. This is much more interesting . . . and fulfilling.'

'I should think they jumped at your application. Did you know Honeypot in the Met?'

The collator's rather stern expression softened into a smile. 'Indeed I did. And now she's a detective super up here. Very popular she was, handing out some very good tips.'

'You mean?'

'On the horses. One of her boyfriends was a trainer. But the tips stopped coming when she married her present husband. Also a super, I believe?'

'Yes. And he's the boss-man around here, so be careful what old tales you spread around.'

Mr Nicholson smiled. 'I'm not much of a gossip. And, if any hints come in while you're out, where can I contact you?'

'Try my car radio.'

NINE

Jane, meanwhile, was having a worse morning than DI Fellowes. After having left the police station, she had been confronted by the usual few clients seeking urgent attention for their pets and by a surgery that had been bloodied by a dying puppy, largely cleared of medications by the knifeman, turned over by the police and partly scrubbed out by Helen Maple until her time ran out. Between advising the clients what prescribed medications to buy from the pharmacy across the Square (in the process sacrificing her own profit on those items) and keeping a record for billing purposes, Jane embarked on a final clean and tidy of the rooms, listing for Ian the missing drugs and at the same time preparing a similar list for her insurers and for reordering, mopping away blood missed by Helen when summoned to stand in at the jeweller's shop, and removing the last traces of fingerprint powders.

The last of the morning callers was an old lady whose parrot had made an escape and was circling above the town. Jane could only advise her to wait for the hungry bird to return home, meanwhile spreading the word in the town that anyone given the opportunity should drop a towel, a coat or a rug over the bird; and no, she would not attempt to dart the bird with tranquillizer because, firstly, she would almost certainly miss and anaesthetize some citizen with the descending missile and, secondly, the bird, if darted, would fall asleep in mid-air and break its neck on crash landing.

Jane had just ushered the old dear out and was preparing to launch a fresh attack on the outstanding jobs when two more figures darkened the doorway carrying between them a bundle of no little weight. With a sinking heart she recognized the Hepworth brothers and she hurried to plant herself in their way.

'No,' she said. 'Bugger off, the pair of you. I told you last time never to come back. Not until it's to bring me a kitten or a budgie or even a spaniel. But this isn't any of those.'

Bart Hepworth shook his balding head. He was a rough-looking man, roughly dressed. His brother, who was smaller and comparatively dapper, had shut the surgery door, greatly reducing the noise of a heavy vehicle passing through the Square, and hung Jane's sign on it.

'No,' Bart said. 'It isn't one of those as you damn well know. It's nothing that you haven't done before.'

'But I'm not going to do it again. I told you.'

Bart waved aside the refusal. 'You wouldn't turn away an injured animal. I know you. And it's against your oath or your professional obligations or something.'

'It's also against the law to do it,' Jane said.

'Not treating a dog,' said the brother. Jane never knew his real name but he was always known as Ossy. 'There's no law says you mustn't treat a dog.'

'There's laws that add up to saying that I mustn't treat a dog that has obviously been wounded in an illegal fight.'

'There's never anything to say that the fight was illegal. It just broke out in the park.'

They had had this argument a dozen times, but now that Jane was an established vet with surgical premises and her name in the *Yellow Pages* she was not going to be persuaded. 'It would be becoming an accomplice,' she said.

Bart grinned, showing broken teeth. 'There's no law about accomplices in Scotland; they have to think up charges like breach of the peace and suchlike, which can't apply to treating a dog. I asked a law student who won fifty quid on this one a fortnight back. This is Borden.' Bart knew very well that once Jane had set eyes on an injured animal she would be unable to turn her back. He stooped and opened the old coat, revealing an unconscious dog of no very certain breed but partly resembling an American pit bull terrier. One side of its body and a foreleg were crusted with blood.

'After Lizzie Borden, I suppose,' Jane said. Bart usually named his dogs after famous killers.

'Aye. Listen, you can't leave the poor bugger to suffer. If you'll not help him I'll have to take my gun and put him down myself. And then I'll tell the cops and the SSPCA of all the times you did it before. That'll put a crimp in your business.'

'You'd be confessing to promoting dogfights.'

'I wouldn't need to confess a damn thing. I'd just be telling what I know.'

'It may not be that bad.' Jane stooped for a good look. 'When did this happen?'

'Last night.'

'And you left the poor devil until now? Hoping the bleeding would stop of its own accord? Lift him through into the surgery. And, you listen to me. This dogfighting has to stop. This is the last time, you hear me?'

'I hear you.'

'I really mean it and next time I shan't weaken. The poor beggar's unconscious – blood loss, I suppose.'

'I always have something to hand,' Bart said. 'Something herbal. But I know what you usually use and I brought . . .' He opened his hand to show a phial and a cardboard package that she recognized as containing a tube.

'Where did you get those?' Jane demanded. 'They look like what was taken from here on Saturday.'

'I knew you'd been done on Sat'day. All over the town, isn't it? This isn't any of your stuff and you can ask at the chemist's yourself. That's where we went. The pharmacist would've wanted prescriptions but Ossy knows one of the girls.'

Jane nodded. The explanation was credible. Ossy probably knew all the girls. Jane could not see it herself but
other females all seemed to go weak at the knees and
everywhere else when he produced his suggestive smirk.

Jane sighed. 'Cash up front,' she said. Interrupted by
only two phone calls, neither of which was urgent, she fell
to work washing and sterilizing the wounds preparatory to
sewing them up.

Once the wounds had been sewn back up and the dog
looked more comfortable in its anaesthesia-induced sleep,
Jane admonished the Hepworth brothers again with a
promise not to fall for their threats next time and hurriedly
ushered them out the door.

Roland was lunching with Simon Parbitter, courtesy of
Simon's wife, so Jane ate alone in the café in the Square.
She had spent more time than she thought she could spare
in mopping up Borden's blood and some remaining traces
from Saturday's puppy; but she had dealt with a short list
of afternoon clients and was tidying up again when Ian's
message arrived, phoned by DS Bright, inviting her to the
police building for another urgent round table.

The former gymnasium had suffered a major change.
More wall had been covered with whiteboard, which in
turn was covered with lists and charts and photographs
with more arriving and being Blu-tacked up by the minute,
in three groups. Many of the photographs had been tactfully trimmed to remove the more scandalous views of the
bride and a woman constable was repeating this process
of censorship with a fresh batch. In many cases such
butchery would have removed the identities of some of the
guests, in which instances the editing was achieved by the
use of a Magic Marker. The woman constable, however,
was limiting herself to scribbling over the gauzy inserts in
the nightdress, producing an effect indistinguishable from
black lace. Most of Ian's little team, which had acquired

two new faces, was assembled in a semicircle fronting on the photograph wall, and were assisting the censorship with advice and comments which ceased abruptly when it was observed that the subject of the photographs had arrived.

'Jane,' Ian said – loudly, in case someone had failed to register her presence – 'come in and take a seat. As the central figure at the wedding you're the person most likely to identify the guests. I'll explain. As near as we can work it out, Knifeman left your surgery at about three-fifty. It is possible that he had some faster form of transport than the supposed bicycle so we're assuming that he could have reached the reception by four. This first block of photographs is of those timed before then. The middle group is of those taken after four. The third batch is of those without the time on them, but it will be possible to time most of them by the context.

'For the moment, we'll confine our interest to the middle group. To save you wasting time and mental energy I may as well tell you that all the photographs have been examined but, as far as can be seen, nobody has shiny hands, so if Knifeman figures here he had already removed the gloves, which makes sense really considering he's trying to blend in at a wedding celebration.

'We'll take a look at anyone who is absent from the early photographs but appears suddenly in the later shots.

'Now, we have already put numbers to the characters and we'll try to give them all identities whenever we can. And by that I mean everybody, not just youngsters in jeans, because anybody may be a witness and they'll all have to be interviewed in due course.'

'And,' said the collator gloomily, 'it will be my pleasure to tabulate everybody's movements to discover who may be able to confirm the alibi of each of the suspect youths over an uncertain period. Isn't life wonderful?' Secretly he was looking forward to a task that could be approached methodically; one that would produce end results that would be seen and appreciated; and which would keep him well away from his wife's demands for as long as it could be spun out.

Jane stood and approached the wall of photographs. 'May we have the lights up, please?' she asked. 'And can you lend me a large magnifier? Where do you want me to write the names and numbers?'

She settled down for an hour's labour. At her suggestion Mr Nicholson took the telephone directory and one of the constables the laptop and they added phone numbers and addresses when they could. Jane was surprised to discover that she could recognize more than half of the densely packed crowd.

Upon reaching the last photograph on the whiteboard, Jane stretched her back and rolled her shoulders, relieved to have finally finished her arduous task. She noticed that Ian was busy on a phone call, so she said a quick goodbye to the collator and the constable who'd been helping her, and made her not unwelcome escape.

TEN

'I suppose,' Jane said to her husband that evening, 'that if there's some weirdie going around threatening people with a sharp knife Ian has to do something about it. And if he's got no other starting point I suppose he has to tackle it whatever way he can. It does seem to me that he's taking a sledgehammer to crack a nut but I don't know what else he could do. He may be getting a kick out of conducting a murder enquiry in miniature, but if it keeps a dozen officious busybodies from haunting the streets and persecuting motorists then it has my support. It just takes up rather a lot of *my* time and mental energy.'

'Hello,' said Roland. 'You've changed your tune. Have you been parking on double yellows again?'

'Only once.' The washing up was finished. Jane, rather red about the face and ears, turned and leaned back against the kitchen worktop, her legs really stiff now after being on her feet with little let-up over the past few hours. 'Doctors get away with parking wherever the car happens to stop. Well, I'm a doctor and my patients are animals who can't even pop into the pharmacy for their own medicines.'

'Nice try, but I doubt if you'll ever get away with it.'

'Both the traffic wardens have dogs. I'm just waiting for the day that one of them tries to cross the road and gets run over and I'll take my time walking from the official car park.'

Roland chuckled. 'You won't and you know it,' he said. 'You could no more leave an animal in pain than you could flap your arms and fly. You'd park beside the injured dog and its owner would prosecute you. How did you get on with Ian's identification parade?'

Jane moved back to a hard kitchen/dining chair. She thought of suggesting a move to the sitting room where she could collapse into a comfortable leather armchair, but the sky had cleared and a low evening sun was slanting in and making the kitchen glow. The sitting room would be dull and probably cold. 'I've got to hand it to Ian,' she said. 'He kept it methodical; and his new collator was right on the ball. I managed to put names to about half the faces in the photographs and our local bobbies added some more. I've identified the young boy's mother, you know the boy who brought in the badly injured puppy on our wedding morning, so they're going to rout out the boy and interview him, just to make sure he's not the culprit, but I'm fairly confident he's not. Anyway, the collator was jumping around, picking up on the people who had been there all morning and knocking them off the list. How he kept track, when each photograph might show ten or twenty people, I don't know; but he seemed to manage. Then I was invited to pick out the physiques and head shapes most resembling what I had said about my attacker, and there I got stuck because my memory was fading to the point that I had stopped being sure what were real memories and which were me remembering things I'd thought since. Am I making sense?'

'As much as you ever do.'

Jane grinned and gave Roland a friendly punch on the shoulder. 'That's all right then. At the same time, the list was being compared with the other list, the one of what we know about Knifeman, which isn't a lot but it was quite possible to remove the very old, the very young, the one-legged or deformed, those with heads of shapes that I would definitely have remembered; and soon, I suppose, Hugh Dodd will be subjected to much the same inquisition. And I'm quite prepared to bet that his list and mine will only fit where they touch.

'And talking of bets,' Jane went on, 'Bart Hepworth and his brother came to the surgery again.'

'With Crippen?'

'I think they've retired Crippen, he'd been in too many bouts. They've got a new one, Borden. Just as chewed up. I tried to tell them to bugger off but it was the same old story. I had to sew up the wounds or they'd spill the beans about all the patch-up jobs I did in the past.'

Roland, whose mind had been at least half on his current writing rather than wholly on his conversation with his wife, returned it to Jane. 'You should have stuck to your guns,' he said. 'They couldn't drop you in the shit without following you in, and deeper. I suspect that it was your sympathy for the dog that motivated you.'

'Well, maybe. He looked at me as though he knew that I was the person who could make the pain go away. Which is a step forward. Usually they look at me as if to say, "Touch me with that needle and I'll have you for dinner".'

Roland turned to face her. 'Now, you listen to me. All right, dogfighting is an offence that quite rightly they take seriously. If you don't patch up the damage, what's going to happen? They try to find another vet. If they can't, and if the dog dies, they'll bury it quietly in the woods. But if the authorities get on to you, what then?'

'I'll tell you something,' Jane said. They were alone but she lowered her voice. 'You know the SSPCA man, the curly-haired one? I put it to him once as a hypothetical question. *If* somebody brought me a dog injured in a fight, what should I do? His answer was perfectly positive. I should treat the dog but call the SSPCA who would notify the police. I pointed out that there was no way to tell whether the injuries had been caused in a street confrontation or an organized fight but he said that that didn't matter, it was for the police to investigate and decide.'

'He'd soon change his tune if you started getting him out of bed for every dog-bite that's brought to you. Anyway, you can deny everything. The Hepworths came to you for the first time and threatened that if you didn't help them they'd make up a story about all the times you'd helped them in the past. Beyond that point you could hide behind medical confidentiality.'

'Which doesn't apply to animals.'

Roland pointed a finger at her and then tapped her on the nose. 'But you've been told that it does.'

She ducked her head aside. 'Who by?'

'By me. I'm wrongly sure of my facts.'

'You crime writers. Always ready with the devious escape. But being wrongly advised about the law has never been an accepted excuse. The sun's going in, let's move through. There's something coming on the telly that I want to see – and those are words that I never dared hope to hear passing my lips again.'

When they had settled in one of the enormous leather chairs, Jane picked up the remote control of the TV, but she hesitated before saying cryptically, 'Something Bart said started me thinking. He mentioned that a law student won around fifty quid or something, betting on Borden, just a couple of weeks ago. That's got me wondering whether there isn't something Bart can do for me . . . I'd like another word with that man before giving up on him.'

ELEVEN

The activities of Knifeman seemed likely to become the prime topic of interest around Newton Lauder, but Jane and Roland were soon taken out of those discussions. The kind of happy chance that occurs too rarely in this life brought together all the elements needed for a perfect and immediate honeymoon. A letter from a big-time art dealer informed Jane that two major collectors had become willing to accept the provenance of the Raeburn painting and had tried to outbid each other. Jane emailed immediate instructions to sell quickly before the white heat of enthusiasm had time to cool.

The postponed honeymoon was now financially possible. At the same time, Jane heard that a colleague with a veterinary practice near Edinburgh had been forced by a serious illness in the family to cancel a planned luxury cruise. The tickets were available as were the services of the locum who had been booked for the period. Their passports were valid.

It was a win-win-win situation. The locum was given the keys to Whinmount and a hasty briefing on such matters as which dog would swallow any item left unattended on the floor and which owner was almost certain to mistake breathed-in fluff for kennel cough. Mr and Mrs Fox were airborne within thirty-six hours.

They joined the ship at Naples. Their cabin was luxurious, the cuisine deserved the maximum number of stars and the Eastern Mediterranean was at its beautiful best. Roland had his laptop with him and was polishing off his outstanding chores for Simon Parbitter while enlarging the scope of his incipient novel. By working several of the Greek island

backgrounds into the plot he hoped to make the whole trip
tax deductible. Jane spent her time reading all the novels
she'd meant to read for the past few years and just never
had the time, as well as perusing various veterinary journals
she'd brought with her, to make sure she was keeping up
with the most up-to-date practices and drugs in the world
of animal medicine. She also spent a certain amount of
time in the self-indulgent pastime of just relaxing and doing
nothing very much at all apart from lying down on beautifully comfortable deck chairs and anticipating how her life
was about to change once the new baby was born – although
it was still a fair few months away – and whether she'd
ever get a moment to put her feet up again! Back to the
present, and Jane's locum had only consulted her by phone
on two or three occasions but stuck strictly to business, so
there wasn't too much to concern herself with regarding
their lives back home. They could truly feel a million miles
away from the mundanities of their normal life.

The other three couples at their dinner table proved
compatible. Conversation was wide ranging but after the
first week was beginning to slow. The subject of mugging
was mentioned. One of the couples was an Irish professor
and his wife. He said that he had been mugged in the street
at Naples. 'And by my own wife,' he added.

His wife, who had a truly Irish temper that her husband
enjoyed triggering, seemed to be on the point of explosion
so Jane decided on a quick change of topic before the
tranquillity of the trip should be endangered. She mentioned
the activities of Knifeman including the insertion of the
microchip. The story of the wedding seemed largely irrele-
vant and she limited herself to a mention of the credit card
slips that had found their way there.

There was an immediate stirring of interest. 'Has anyone
been arrested?' the professor's wife asked.

'They hadn't up to when we left home, a week ago
yesterday,' Jane said.

'And you haven't phoned up to ask?' said the husband of the youngest couple in tones of amazement. Jane suspected that they also were honeymooners. 'But you must. Why not ring up now?'

'Knowing wouldn't change anything,' Roland said. 'We'll hear all about it when we get home.'

'But *we* won't,' the young man's even younger wife pointed out. 'Go on, phone.'

'My phone's locked in the safe in our cabin,' Jane said. 'I check it once a day for voicemail and that's quite enough. In my job the phone only brings bad news so I can do without it on . . . on holiday.'

The young wife reached into her husband's pocket. 'Use this one.'

There was a murmur of agreement around the table. Jane bowed to the will of the majority, only too well aware that the cost of mobile phone calls to Britain from abroad approached the cost of brain surgery without NHS support. She keyed in a well-remembered number and found Ian at home. The phone was loud and the others could hear him say that, no, there had been no arrest yet. They were looking into the possibility of getting more sensitive micro-wave detectors. 'I'm glad you called,' he carried on. 'I was hesitating whether to call you. There was an attempt to break into your house but the intruder was chased away by the combination of your dog and your locum.' And how was Jane enjoying her honeymoon?

Damn and blast! She terminated the call as quickly as she could without downright rudeness.

'So you're newly-weds!' said the professor's wife. 'How sweet!'

'Not as sweet as all that,' said Jane. 'We had been part-ners for a year or more.' She hurried on, hoping to put that admission behind them, and told the story of the wedding, the puppy and the wedding gown. Hilarity reduced most of the table to tears of mirth. The professor's wife's vision became so blurred that she blew her nose on her napkin. The transparency of the nightdress Jane did not dwell on.

The company remained more interested in Knifeman. The professor turned out to have some knowledge of micro-chip technology. 'Your friend the detective inspector needn't waste his time looking for more sensitive detectors. The fault isn't in the detectors. Those little microchips for implanting have to be small enough to spare the animal discomfort. They don't have to be powerful enough to register at any distance, not like the transponders they put on a wild animal to track its movements.'

The other young husband was similarly knowledgeable but disagreed. 'I don't think the microchip could have a power source of its own. It would receive an incoming signal and use that to power the reply. A boosted signal would be all you'd need.'

'I'll tell Ian.'

It would have been a pity to be in touch with so much, if discordant, expertise without exploiting it. When she asked the question the two men were agreed that lead foil under the shirt would be enough to negate the signal.

'But just fancy being on those sort of terms with a police inspector!' said the professor's wife. She had shown signs of IRA sympathies. 'What would a burglar be looking for in your house? Do you think it's connected to the burglary at your surgery?'

Jane and Roland had already agreed to avoid mentioning the supposed Raeburn painting. 'I don't suppose that there's a connection with Knifeman,' Roland said. 'Probably an opportunist thief who thought the house would be empty.' It had been a leading question. Surely, he thought, the professor's wife could not be in league with a team of burglars and looking for information about valuables; but you never knew. The IRA was reputed to have links with organized crime. 'Of course,' he added, 'the inspector may have spread the word of our absence as a trap.' *You can spread that around and welcome,* he thought.

With the agreement of the telephone's owner he called Ian again. 'I suppose the house is in turmoil?' he said. 'Everything upside down and fingerprint powder everywhere?' There was an embarrassed silence from the other end. 'Do us a favour,' Roland said. 'Ask Helen Maple to clean the house for us – at our expense,' he added quickly before Ian could rush to the defence of his budget. Further inspiration hit him. 'And would you mind asking Helen whether she'd like to take on light housekeeping duties for us, say three mornings a week at the going rate.'

'What brought that on?' Jane asked when the call had finished and the other couples were engaged in a new conversation of their own.

Roland shrugged. 'We're both working now. You're becoming stressed and that's not good for the baby, or for you, and I'm not clever at domestic things. We can afford some help, so let's have it.'

Jane felt her heart swell with love. At last he was thinking of her. It was unlikely to last but the most difficult part of any process is to begin it.

TWELVE

Jane and Roland returned home tanned, relaxed and with renewed energy. Roland's laptop was loaded with ideas, snatches and whole chapters of works that he was determined to plunge ahead with. Jane's locum had earned her one or two bad marks by mistaken diagnoses but at least he had walked Sheba and, with Helen's help, had left the house and the surgery almost clean and fairly tidy. Sheba, the young Labrador, was suspicious of these newcomers for a few minutes and then, when recognition surfaced, went half mad with joy at their return.

It took only a day to restore the familiar muddle. Soon, Roland was engrossed in printouts. Jane, for her part, found that some clients had put off consulting the locum about lumps and limps until they could get Jane's personal attention, even if they had to wait for an appointment some days ahead. Jane was in the middle of breaking the worst possible news to a devoted cat owner when Ian telephoned.

'I am sorry,' Jane told him, sounding more stressed than sorry. The relaxing effect of a holiday seldom lasts much longer than the journey home. 'If you want to jump the queue and take priority over all my other customers, you'll have to arrest me. I am a busy professional and my first responsibilities are to my clients. I quite understand that the victim of a crime is only a bloody nuisance with few if any rights, but if you want to treat me as a witness you can make an appointment and send somebody to see me at home.'

Ian sighed audibly. 'I'll come myself this evening, eightish. See you then at Whinmount.'

Jane disconnected grumpily. She had rather been enjoying bossing a fairly senior policeman around.

Promptly at eight, Ian Fellowes arrived at the door of Whinmount. The day was cold and damp, a shock to the system after the Greek islands. One of the few alterations that Jane had made since inheriting the house had been to have the garage added with a covered way to a side door. The covered way also acted as a *porte cochère*. Ian was therefore able to reach the house dry. Jane took him into the sitting room where Roland was already seated with a pad on his knee, drafting more ideas for his novel, a murder mystery in which the victim was pushed into a volcano on Santorini. Upon Ian's entrance into the room, the future blockbuster was laid aside.

Ian was always willing to extend his hours of duty but he was just as flexible about other rules. He accepted a small Scotch. 'You must be busy after skiving off for a fortnight or more,' he said to them both, 'but we've struggled along without you. Now comes the time for catching up. Have you remembered any more facts, presences, descriptions, anything that might help us?'

'Not a thing,' Jane said.

Roland grunted agreement but added the words of advice from their table companions on the cruise.

'I had already gleaned those fragments of information elsewhere,' Ian said. 'Have you thought of anything that somebody, Knifeman in particular, might have wanted to get from this house?'

'Same answer,' Roland said.

'Then I may as well start updating you. There was another attack while you were away disporting yourselves. That's why I didn't come down to see you at your surgery, Jane. We've been passing it off as an accident. We don't want the news to leak out for fear of copycat crime – which as far as we know we haven't got yet.'

Roland and Jane sat dumbly for a few seconds. Then Jane said, 'Had this already happened when I spoke to you from the ship? And was anybody hurt?'

'And if so, who?' Roland asked.

Ian sighed. 'Yes, it had happened the previous day but I wasn't going to broadcast the story and I'll be grateful if you talk about it as little as possible. Do you know Minnie Pilrig?'

'Plumpish lady?' Jane said. 'Late middle age? Acts as stand-in shop assistant for several shopkeepers?'

Ian raised his eyebrows. Jane had erred on the charitable side. Minnie was elderly and had passed beyond plumpish to definitely fat, but no doubt Jane was doing as she would be done by. 'That's the one,' he confirmed. 'She was looking after my father-in-law's shop. The strict orders laid down by his partner, the money man, are that all cash bar the one-hundred-pound float goes into the night safe at the bank when closing up each evening. It was dusk and Knifeman was waiting on the doorstep when she stepped out to go across to the bank. She tried to hang on to the bag and got a cut face as a reward.'

'That's a shame,' Jane said. 'Such a cheery person, with a smile and a kind word for everybody.'

'She's a chatterbox,' Ian said, frowning. Clearly the age-old dichotomy between the sexes was at work. 'Anyway, she isn't dead yet, nor likely to be. She's in the cottage hospital here, rather sorry for herself and very vocal about what she'll get her nephew to do to Knifeman if they catch him.'

'She'd better not hold her breath,' Jane said. 'Her nephew delivers our milk and he jumps at shadows.'

'Good!' Ian said. 'We can do without a lot of vigilantes around here. The worry is that it seems our attacker is trying his – or her – hand at different methods of extracting money any way they can. A doorstep mugging – with violence this time – is a phase beyond what they've done so far, thank goodness, but it either shows the need for money is getting more acute, or they're getting a taste for it. Both reasons are worrying for us considering we have no ideas as to the identity yet. And Mrs Pilrig wasn't much help in that area. Her description of her attacker was beyond belief.'

'Your father-in-law won't be pleased,' Roland said.

'That he is not. Luckily there was only about three hundred in cash in the bag – sometimes it may be several times that – but his insurers are being sticky because he let Mrs Pilrig carry so much money without any protection. He wants me to speak to them for him because, after all, it is we police who discourage armed bodyguards. That's the gospel according to my revered father-in-law.'

'And to think,' said Jane, 'that I was on the point of asking him to guard me whenever I go to the night safe.'

'But you're not a criminal,' Roland said. 'Only the criminal is allowed to defend himself.'

Ian looked indignant but refused to rise to the bait. It was an old argument and Jane made little use of the night safe anyway.

Jane was uncertain whether, in not reporting her knowledge about dogfighting, she was committing a crime, so Roland's comment put an end to her part in the discussion.

'How badly marked is Mrs Pilrig?' Roland asked. 'Is her beauty spoiled for ever?'

Jane contented herself with a 'Humpf!' but Ian said, 'She'll have a scar, no doubt about it. She says that if she was a man she'd pass it off as a duelling scar.'

'Is she getting visitors?' Roland asked.

'One or two. Keith had arrived back from delivering a very expensive rifle just seconds after it happened and he lifted her into the shop and called the ambulance. The Square was empty at the time with everybody having their tea in front of the telly, so the drama passed unobserved. We've been calling it an accidental fall against a boot-scraper. We asked her to keep it that way and she's been having fun phoning her friends and relations and passing on the same tale, gradually elaborating the story until it's getting near the borderline of credibility. But we'll have to let the truth out soon so that people will know to be even more careful.' Ian made a face. 'We just don't know what comes next. Does he take fright and stop or, now that he's drawn blood, will he get a taste for it and look for another victim? We can't guess. Psychologists employed by the police have gone beyond reality so often that nobody believes them any more.

'Peeling away the exaggerations occasioned by a dramatic attack on an imaginative old lady, Mrs Pilrig gave us pretty much the same description as you did, Jane, and the Dodd boy. She gave us one extra piece of information, a rather uncertain piece. She thinks that she smelled after-shave on him, the commonest one around here. The chemist says it's the one that all the women give their menfolk at Christmas if they can't think of anything else, so it doesn't carry us much further forward except to suggest that Knifeman is probably male.'

'That's not exactly conclusive,' Jane said. 'When I get a spot – it doesn't happen often, thank God, just now and again – I give it a dab with Roland's aftershave. The alcohol in it seems to be the best there is for drying up a pimple.'

'I'll pass that tip on to my nephew,' Ian said. 'His life's being made miserable by teenage acne at the moment.'

'Tell him that it only lasts about five years, ten at the most,' Roland said. 'That should cheer him up.'

'You're evil,' said his wife. 'Evil.'

'Does that bother you?'

'Not a lot. Not when you're only evil with me.' Roland and Jane smirked at each other, being rather amused by the direction of the conversation. Ian, on the other hand, thought it was probably time to take his leave and departed Whinmount promptly.

THIRTEEN

The successor to the jeweller for whom the surgery had originally been built was now only a few doors further along the Square. Central to that window and outshining a display of cheap watches and chromium plated cutlery, for the previous few weeks a necklace of three strands of pearls had glowed discreetly on a base of black velvet sculpted after the manner of a female neck. It was rumoured that a certain lady, wife of a prominent politician and chatelaine of a castle tucked away in a glen many kilometres away from Newton Lauder, had sold this wedding present to the jeweller in order to raise funds to settle a gambling debt. Whatever the truth or otherwise of the rumour, the necklace had been written up in a glossy magazine so there could be no doubt about the genuineness of its components.

Jane would not have been lured from the path of virtue by any diamond on earth, a girl's best friend or not, but she admitted to herself that she did have a thing for pearls. Even the sale of the Raeburn painting would not have enabled the purchase of these perfectly matched and graded jewels, but she did yearn secretly for the lovely thing on the rare occasions when she dropped her takings into the night safe at the bank. This she might do on one evening a week when there was enough cash to merit the precaution. Jane never held a clinic on a Saturday, reserving it, along with occasional weekdays, as her day for making calls at farms, so on some Friday evenings she made that pilgrimage.

On a Friday ten days after her return from honeymoon, Jane walked past the jeweller's window, keeping her eyes stonily averted rather than pause where Knifeman might fancy a second attack on her. At the bank a certain dexterity amounting to sleight of hand was called for because it was her custom to carry a decoy package openly while the real cash was hidden in a less bulky but much more valuable envelope in her underwear. Fumbling inside her coat and the waistband of her skirt she retrieved it, posting it through the night safe slot and replacing it with the decoy package.

On the return trip, walking carefully for fear of displacing the thick envelope, she felt free to pause for a lustful glance in the jeweller's window; and she was immediately uneasy. Black clouds, which had seemed to be a feature of that so-called summer, had covered the sky; dusk seemed to have arrived hours early but it was too soon for street lights and the jeweller's shop was generally the brightest thing in the Square. The necklace had vanished from the window.

Jane had met the jeweller, Mr Golspie – a shrewd old man with a beaming smile and several gold teeth – on the doorstep of the bank only the previous day and he had said that he planned to send the necklace to a jewellery fair in London in a month's time. Until then, it would continue to be a draw for customers who called to admire but often lingered to purchase something closer to their means.

So perhaps he had changed his mind in sudden fear of a robbery. Or perhaps the robbery had happened. She tried the shop door but the night latch was locked. Mr Golspie's habit when closing for the night was to turn down the shop's lights to the minimum required to intrigue potential customers and to expose any burglar to public view; and this was the routine when he left early. Of recent years he had taken to heading for his home whenever Helen Maple, his occasional assistant, was available in good time from her other and very varied commitments, but the same rule applied. Tonight the lights were at full strength although there was nobody to be seen behind the sparkling counter or at the little desk where watch batteries were changed.

Jane had her mobile phone in her pocket. She keyed for emergency services, was connected to the police station only a few hundred yards away and reported that something seemed to be wrong at the jeweller's shop. Back at her surgery, she got rid of her dummy package in a drawer, collected the knife that she used for opening envelopes and returned to Mr Golspie's shop.

There she waited and waited. The police, it seemed, did not attach much weight to her unease. The recessed doorway gave her some shelter from a cold breeze. After twenty minutes she took out her phone again and called Ian's office number. The DI knew Jane's character well and understood that she was not given to false alarms. Within three or four minutes she saw his sturdy form approaching.

'Tell me what's wrong,' he said.

Jane explained. 'What's more,' she added, 'you can see that only the Yale-type night latch is locked. The proper lock, mortise I think it's called, hasn't been turned. Mr Golspie is never so careless and nor is Helen Maple. I think we should go in.' Ian nodded and began to feel in his pocket. Jane produced her letter knife. 'This should do it,' she said.

Ian took the knife from her and with little difficulty slipped back the cylinder night latch. The door opened. There was no bell – the shop was a single room so no bell was necessary. A muffled sound fetched them both forward to look behind the counter. Helen Maple was lying there, hidden from the street. Jane's heart was in her mouth but after a single second it was clear that she was not seriously hurt. There were traces of blood from several small stab wounds, little more than scratches, to her face and neck, but she was mainly incapacitated by what appeared to be a common clothes line. Her wrists and ankles were tied and linked together. A yellow duster was folded, slipped between her teeth and tied there with several turns of the same clothes line, pulled tight.

Jane stooped. She was about to begin the process of untying Helen but Ian stopped her. 'The knots can sometimes tell an expert a lot,' he said. Jane twitched the other's skirt down. It seemed to be the least that she could do. Ian produced his miniature camera from his pocket and took two or three shots. Then, with his own penknife, he cut the rope and removed the gag. He went to work on the other ropes.

Helen's first reaction on being freed was of furious anger. She sat up, rubbing her wrists where the skin was marked, and uttered several epithets which were evidently about her assailant. 'He didn't care if I was left there all night,' she said. 'And Mr Golspie opens late on a Saturday morning.'

Ian and Jane helped her up and into the customers' chair. 'Tell me what happened,' Ian said.

Helen was bent forward to rub her ankles. Her voice seemed to be choked off by the cramped position. 'The shops were shutting,' she said at last. 'I was just going to close up. The Square was deserted. Then this man came in. He had a black hood on. And a knife. He made me lie down on the floor and when I was too slow for him he jabbed me with the knife. Och, look at the state of me. There's blood on the blouse my mam gave me for my birthday. She'll be fizzing.' There were tears on Helen's face but whether these were for her blouse or arose out of sheer aggravation Jane could only guess.

A uniformed constable arrived in the doorway. It was his bad luck that he was sent to respond to Jane's phone call and so drew down on himself the full wrath of a detective inspector who was on the lookout for someone to bite. Ian's expressions of contempt for the belated response were still at an early stage when Jane slipped out and collected some sticking plasters and lint from her surgery. Ian was still in good voice when she returned so she set about cleaning and patching Helen's small wounds.

The constable was soon able to share Ian's displeasure with his sergeant, who arrived to discover what was keeping his subordinate. (*A trouble shared is a trouble doubled*, Jane thought to herself.) It was some little time before Ian was satisfied that he had expressed himself adequately on the subject of a forty-minute delay in responding to an emergency call, especially after his own messages had demanded that he be informed immediately of any events possibly linked to Knifeman. He had not managed to extract any explanation for the delay and so he put it down to mere inertia. If he had been told the truth, which was that the uniformed branch had resented being told their jobs by a plain clothes inspector, he might have suffered a seizure.

By this time Mr Golspie had been called back to his shop and was added to the audience while Helen repeated her story. He took the loss of the necklace philosophically being, as he said, fully insured.

Ian Fellowes was at last able to demand Helen's description of her assailant. Helen had now dried her eyes and pulled herself together. She had passed from the tongue-tied state to a garrulous one. Stripped of all repetitions, contradictions and complaints, she described her attacker as being a lot taller than herself (and Helen was taller than average for her age and sex), sturdily built and wearing the aforementioned hood, the customary blue jeans, a denim jacket and polished, black shoes. Ian managed to enquire, without putting words into her mouth, whether he had been wearing any sort of gloves and she said not. Ian, without missing a word of this diatribe, set about preserving any surfaces that the robber might have touched.

Jane was by now late for her evening meal and had little hope that Roland would have begun preparations for it, and Helen, whose job description included making a start to preparing their dinner on the days when she gave domestic help at Whinmount, was fully engaged. But Helen had cast Jane in the role of rescuer and had a grip on her sleeve so that Jane was forced to linger. However, it turned out that Helen lived in digs and that her landlady would be expecting her; so Ian delegated the constable to escort her home while turning his own attention to a last few scathing remarks to the sergeant. Jane made her escape with a muttered promise to call at the incident room next morning.

'Eight sharp,' Ian said and continued in the same breath expressing his opinion of officers who paused for a cup of tea, a chat or even an afternoon nap before responding to an emergency call. The sergeant was sweating big drops and it was not a warm day.

Jane, having little expectation of being given priority or consideration in the morning, paused at her surgery to postpone, by telephone, her first appointment with an ailing calf at a local smallholding. *Behold*, she told herself, *the first shall be last*. She had been at the sort of school where attendance at chapel is compulsory. She called at the local 'takeaway' for a supply of scampi and chips for two.

Just as she had supposed, Jane rose early and arrived at the incident room on the dot of eight only to have to wait through Ian's briefing of his growing team. Ian might be a friend and a police officer but he was also a public servant and Jane had no intention of being penalized by the delusion, common in certain professions, that other people's time came free. The Knifeman situation seemed to have changed very little. She got to her feet and said that her second appointment was almost due but that she would contact him again later, when he was not so busy.

There was no audible gasp at such *lese-majesty* but there was a stiffening to attention in the room as a lesson was absorbed by some and rejected by others.

Ian had been preoccupied, caught up in his own ordered thoughts. He snapped back into reality and saw Jane as a person. 'I'm sorry,' he said with every sign of sincerity. 'Give me a quick outline of anything you can contribute and we'll go into the details later.'

Jane nodded slowly in what she hoped would be taken for a regal bow. 'I was waiting for my last client of the day,' she said, 'a man with a spaniel due to have stitches removed. I postponed it again to be here this morning. While I waited – and then took the phone call putting the appointment off until this morning – I was looking out of the window. As soon as I had had that phone call I went out to the night safe and as I was coming back I noticed that all was not well.

'The shops were shutting and everyone had headed home for their evening meal. There was no foot traffic except for three people who passed my window on foot. I kept looking out of the window because whenever I heard footsteps I expected it to be the owner of the spaniel. But two of those were women, hurrying home to dish up high tea – Mrs Murtry and Mrs Haven. They both live in flats in what you might call the blind corner of the Square, by which I mean the corner that has no entry into it, not even a footpath. Between them the ladies have two cats, three hamsters and a Belgian hare, which is how I come to know them. The third was a young man, although this person was crossing the Square so he didn't walk directly past my window. And, to be honest, I didn't pay him much attention because I was more interested in when I might be able to get home for my own dinner – which, thankfully, would have been a quickie, being fish. As it worked out, I had to get a takeaway of scampi and chips from Spiretti's. Also, he could have been fairly typical of the young men of the town that I hardly noticed him at all. He was coming from the direction of Mr Golspie's shop and from what little I noticed of him he had the sort of build and head shape of the man who robbed me and he was dressed much the same, but that may be partly hindsight.'

One of the plain-clothes constables raised a hand. 'It was a very dark afternoon. Did you have your surgery lights on?'

'I see what you're getting at,' Jane said. 'No, I'd just put them out, ready to walk along to the night safe. He wouldn't have known that I was there. And now I must go. If there are any more questions let me know and I'll come back at a better time. But the significant thing that I wanted to draw to your attention is that my initial thoughts are that he was rather unlike Helen Maple's description of her attacker, so might not have had anything to do with it at all. Good afternoon.'

Ian glanced up at the clock on the wall. 'Afternoon is still several hours away,' he said. Jane only smiled. She had made her point.

FOURTEEN

When Ian visited Jane's surgery on the Monday afternoon he found her alone, waiting for that bane of her life – a client who was late for an appointment. In this one instance there was some excuse for the tardiness. The client had no car and her dog had had a leg amputated. The dog, a collie/Labrador cross, still enjoyed life and was a keen and willing walker but he was inevitably slowed.

Ian's immediate question was: 'Are you sure that the young man you saw pass your window had to be Helen Maple's attacker?'

Jane glanced around the comfortable familiarity of her surgery while she thought about it. 'Well, as I said yesterday, on first thoughts, no. But having dwelt on it overnight, I'm now not so sure . . .' Jane mulled over the question once again before continuing. 'According to what Helen Maple said, it's the only way the times could fit. She said that he was gone not more than ten minutes before I rattled at the door. Then she heard me go away and she thought that she was going to be there all night. When she heard me come back again she wept tears of relief. What does she say?'

Ian sighed. 'I haven't taxed her with it yet. I just wanted to be quite sure about your evidence.'

'I hope I'm wrong,' Jane said. 'Helen's polite and well behaved and I think she may be good-hearted, though I've sometimes suspected her of being a little bit sly, but who isn't? In a stressful situation one tends to remember things as being larger than life.' Jane lost eye contact with Ian and looked over his shoulder while she thought. 'I was called in once to dart and tranquillize a gorilla that had escaped from a zoo. It was a female, quite young and small. And she genuinely liked people and was quite hurt when they all screamed and ran away. She stood about four and a half feet maximum but every witness put her at well over six feet tall. Helen could be making an honest mistake. I can't go further than to say that the man who passed near my window was of ordinary height. I see people passing every day and on average their heads just come up to the dormer windows on the other side of the Square. I'd have noticed anything different.'

'I'll tread carefully,' Ian said.

'Do that. What's been annoying me is that his general outline looked familiar without having an identity, if you know what I mean. I have a feeling that if I'd actually looked at his face I'd have known him and I might have solved the whole case for you. If his face was uncovered; but I didn't even notice that. Maybe I'm kidding myself.'

'It does happen,' Ian said. Jane could see that his mind was working furiously.

The next few days passed in a routine fashion for Jane, hers and Roland's life now back to normal after their wedding and honeymoon. Jane's waistline was slowly expanding, as it tends to do when a baby is thriving inside, and thankfully she wasn't feeling too exhausted yet with her busy veterinary practice and looking after a grateful yet not wholly house-trained husband.

On the Thursday evening of that week there was yet another visit from Ian. He arrived at the door of Whinmount and asked for a private word with Jane. Roland, visibly offended, took Sheba for a walk. Jane took Ian into the sitting room and offered him a drink but he shook his head, thanking her politely. 'I feel I have to keep a clear mind. I seem to be tiptoeing over a tightrope, quite a long way above the ground. I spoke to young Helen.' He ground to a halt.

'And?' Jane prompted.

'And at first she was indignant. I didn't mention your name—'

'Thank you for that.'

'You'd asked me not to. I just said that a witness had seen a man arriving at the shop and that he had to be the attacker because of the times, but that he did not resemble the description she had given us. I've had quite a lot of practice in dealing with witnesses who try to tell fibs and I could see that she was lying. She tried to bluster and she tried tears and I told her that she could have a solicitor present if she so wished, or it needn't be a solicitor, she could have a friend or relation with her. She brightened up at that and asked if she could have you.'

'Me?' Jane squeaked. 'Why me, for God's sake? I hardly know the girl except to employ her occasionally.'

'Well, she doesn't have any relatives here and she knows you and it was quite obvious yesterday that she looked on you as her rescuer. After all, you did see the signs and figure out that something was wrong and then you stuck to your guns, saving her from a night of great discomfort if nothing worse.'

Jane laughed. 'But I'll tell you in advance and for nothing that I'm not going to worm my way into her confidence and then come running to you with her story.'

Ian laughed aloud. 'This is why I decided to approach you myself instead of sending Bright. You've been watching too much television. If you agree to be her moral support it would be in absolute confidence unless she said otherwise. If you think that she would be better to tell the truth, try to convince her that, that's all I ask.'

Jane thought it over for a full minute and then nodded. 'All right.'

'You'll do it? Good! What time are you free tomorrow?'

'I always try to keep the last hour of the morning free in case of emergencies.'

Ian raised one eyebrow. 'Emergencies always happen just before lunch?'

'Don't be more of an ass than nature intended,' Jane said severely. 'If I've had a morning emergency I can catch up during that hour. If one happens in the afternoon I can stay a little late. And if we have a day without emergencies, or occurrences that owners think are emergencies, which are all too rare – a day without them, I mean – I use the time to make doubly sure that everything's clean and tidy and sterile. I take it that bang goes my clean-and-boil period tomorrow?'

'Would you please come up to the nick at twelve tomorrow?'

'Had you not better see if Helen's free then?'

'She'll be free if I have to free her.' Ian's tone suggested that his patience was running out and that it was time for the public to learn that criminal investigations took precedence over personal concerns.

The next morning, Jane was putting on her wax-proofed Barbour coat (another legacy from GG) and was almost out the door when Ian caught her on the phone. 'I'm just coming,' she said irritably. 'I do not forget appointments. I may be slightly late if the patient bleeds or bites me—'

'You are reliability personified,' Ian said. 'You are well known for it. I wish others were the same. Helen Maple has done a runner.'

'You're sure?'

It was Ian's turn to be irritable. 'Nobody has seen her all morning. She didn't turn up at the job she was booked for. What else?'

'She could have been kidnapped. Or murdered. Or have fallen into the canal.'

'God forbid. You could be right, but why would anybody wish to kill or kidnap the victim of a Knifeman robbery?'

A huge articulated vehicle ground its way through the Square. Discussion had to be suspended, which did at least give Jane time to think. While she was thinking she filled the kettle and set it to boil. She might have time for lunch after all. 'Conversely,' she said when the rumble had faded into the distance, 'why would the victim of a Knifeman robbery feel the need to do a runner? I think that both questions may deserve the same answer.'

'That is exactly what I'm afraid of. You mean that she recognized her attacker.'

'That's what I mean. Or, hoping for the best, perhaps she thought that she recognized the robber but was wrong.' While she spoke, Jane was one-handedly unwrapping the parcel of sandwiches that, not knowing when or where she might have the chance of a little lunch, she had brought with her that morning.

Ian made a pained sound that needed no words. 'That idea could open up several whole cans of worms. Would you happen to know whether she has a boyfriend?'

'Only by guesswork. When I'm packing up or leaving for home I've sometimes seen a male figure, late teens or early twenties to judge from the way he carried himself, hovering on the pavement outside the jeweller's shop.' The kettle came to the boil. She poured a mug of coffee. 'It could well have been a boyfriend waiting for her to come off duty. I'm sorry, Ian. If I'd known that he was going to figure in a crime case or if I'd thought that he was waiting for me I'd have paid more attention.'

'You're a respectable married woman now,' Ian said. 'You should put such thoughts out of your head. I can't get hold of her landlady just now but she should know whether there's a boyfriend.'

The call finished. Jane went to work on her sandwiches. Only ten minutes later she was interrupted by the entry of a stout, white-haired woman in a white lambswool coat. She was unaccompanied by any pet, which was unusual for visitors to the surgery.

'I'm Mrs Black,' the woman announced.

Jane was not always good at names and faces but she thought that she would remember Mrs Black because the name was so remarkably inappropriate.

'You're Miss Highsmith?' the lady enquired.

'I was,' Jane said. 'I've been Mrs Fox for the last few weeks but I haven't had time to change the name on the door.'

'I'll send my man down, the morn. He's a signwriter to trade. You know Helen Maple? I have two young ladies as lodgers and she's one of them.' Mrs Black was well spoken and her accent was very faint. She was respectably, rather than smartly, dressed, but Jane got the impression that she would not leave her bedroom until she was as neat as a shop window dummy.

'I know Helen, but not very well. She comes and cleans for me.'

'Is that right? She told me about the attack in the shop and being left tied up. She said that she had you to thank for not being left there all night. And she said that she'd asked for you to be with her when she makes a statement to the police today. So I thought I'd best let you know that there's no sign of her this morning and her bed hadn't been slept in.'

'That was thoughtful of you,' Jane said. 'But I was just leaving to meet her at the police station when I had a call to say that she seemed to have vanished and that you weren't at home either.'

Mrs Black seemed flummoxed for a moment but soon recovered her poise. 'Will you be seeing them? I'm supposed to be going to spend a few days with my sister in Coldstream. We've been at the shopping centre in Loanhead all morning. I've left food in the house for both of my charges but I dare say Maggie – the other girl – will get through it. I'll be back on Wednesday, tell them. And this came for her this morning.' There was a frenzied tooting from the Square. 'That's my sister now. I must run.'

'Wait. Mr Fellowes wants most particularly to know if she has a boyfriend.'

'She's been seeing a boy. She's soppy about him but I've never set eyes on him, except once when he rang the doorbell and I looked out of the lounge window. He was . . .'

'Yes?'

'Very ordinary looking. I decided I wouldn't have him if he came in a lucky bag.' The tooting recurred. Mrs Black thrust an envelope into Jane's hands and scuttled out of the door.

Jane brushed away the crumbs from her lunch, washed her coffee mug and then picked up the phone. She caught Ian at his desk. 'I've just had a visit from Helen's landlady,' she told him. 'Helen's been gone since yesterday evening.'

'I knew that—'

'Just hush a moment and listen. I can see my next patient coming across the Square. Helen's landlady, Mrs Black, will be away for a few days but a letter came for Helen this morning.'

'There may be an address—'

'I said to hush. There's one of those little stickers on a corner of it, the ones they give you a whole page of with a charity appeal so that you'll feel obliged to send them some money. It's from a Mrs Hemiston with an address in Morningside. It would give you a starting point.'

'May I speak now? I'll send somebody down for it.'

'And Helen does have a boyfriend. She saw him once from a window. The landlady, I mean. She said that he looked very ordinary and she wouldn't have him if he came with trading stamps. Next client just arriving,' Jane finished hastily and disconnected.

Minutes later she was giving her attention to a parrot with suspected psittacosis. The three-legged dog had lost its place in the queue. Well, it was a tough old world and the handicapped were usually left behind.

FIFTEEN

That evening, Ian made another one of his sudden appearances at Whinmount. Roland was out, conferring with Simon Parbitter, so Jane had the house and Ian to herself. Once again, Ian accepted a small whisky and a chair in the sitting room which was cheered by a log fire in the grate.

'I opened that letter to Miss Maple,' he began.

Jane was mildly shocked. Forgetting for a moment the special responsibilities of the police she remembered instead the sanctity of other peoples' mail. 'Should you have?'

'Yes, I should,' Ian snapped. 'She's a witness and I have reason to believe that she's holding back evidence concerning the identity of Knifeman.'

'Sorry. You're quite right. You're taking this case very seriously, aren't you?'

'Yes, I am. Once somebody starts using a weapon there's no knowing where it will end. If it's a firearm it may turn out to be a toy or a replica, or if it's real there may be no ammunition for it. But a knife is a knife and it's always ready for use. Some day somebody will provoke him, there will be blood and he'll be on the down-slope. Yes, I'm taking this case very seriously indeed. So I opened the letter. To judge from the references to other relations, this Mrs Hemiston is her cousin and they seem to be on very good terms, but she's moved recently and Directory Enquiries doesn't have a new number for her. I thought of getting Edinburgh City Police to make contact, but then I changed my mind.'

'Why was that?'

'You may well ask,' Ian said, more lightly. 'I'm not even quite sure, but I had a gut feeling that Helen Maple was very nervous. She felt vulnerable about something. She might have gone to visit her cousin in order to keep a low profile, as they say, and the arrival of a couple of large, strange coppers on the doorstep might be enough to put her to flight again. If that's where she is, and I have little more to go on than inspired guesswork, I have nothing whatever to persuade Edinburgh to hold her on. So I phoned Honeypot – that's Detective Superintendent Laird to you.'

Jane had never taken kindly to being condescended to. 'I do know Honeypot, thank you very much. She came here in connection with GG's death and some other occasion, you may remember. And she's gone back to using her maiden name because her husband also made superintendent, so she's Superintendent Potterton to us mortals. Strictly speaking, Potterton-Phipps, but Deborah says that she got fed up at having such a long signature. What did you ask of her?'

Ian had turned a little pink at being corrected on the subject of his own superior. 'She had discreet enquiries made of neighbours and it was reported that a young lady arrived there yesterday evening and was not seen to leave. That's as far as we've got so far.'

Jane's hackles began to stir. 'And you are telling me this, why?'

'Your surgery does not open on Saturday or Sunday—'

'A vet's surgery is never closed. I'm on call all the time.'

Ian pretended not to hear. 'I don't want her running off again. I'd like to send a female officer, one with a nice, soothing manner, to interview her with you going along for reassurance. Try to persuade her that it's in her own best interest to speak out.'

'If it is.'

Ian adopted the voice most often used on squalling infants. 'The longer she keeps a secret the more she's endangering herself and possibly others. Will you keep that in mind?'

'If I go.'

He looked at her through narrowed eyes. 'I think you'll go.'

Jane wondered whether he was judging by her usual willingness to help the forces of law and order or by her growing curiosity. 'I suppose I'll have to,' she said. 'Luckily I've nothing booked for tomorrow that can't wait a week. Do I get the police mileage rate? Presumably you won't be sending us in a liveried police car or she'd be out of the back door and running before we reached the doorbell.'

'Take your car. Your companion will fill the tank, on the police account.'

'That's acceptable, just. Who will it be?'

'I don't know yet. Be ready to leave at six tomorrow morning. I'm sorry about the hour—'

'A vet's office is never closed.'

'So you said. You forgive me, then. That's good. I'll have your company dropped on your doorstep. She'll be fully briefed.'

Roland grumbled until he realized that he would be free to stay in bed for as long as he liked and he could then count on being fed by Mrs Parbitter who had a soft spot for him. Jane left him dozing and was washing her breakfast dishes when the slam of a car door followed by a ring at the doorbell announced her visitor. She dried her hands and went to the door.

Ian's selection, or possibly the volunteer, was a young but motherly looking woman. In a pleasant Highland lilt, she introduced herself as Marie Webb, Constable – 'Do call me Marie.' She was wearing a nylon mackintosh over a tweed coat, which seemed to provide for whatever the weather might bring. Her shoes managed to combine comfort with at least a degree of smartness. She was carrying a briefcase which looked at first glance to be fat but light, suggesting that she had brought necessities in case of an overnight stay. Jane was glad that she had had the same forethought though she had no intention of staying away if it could possibly be avoided. She picked up the computer bag, left over from a laptop that she had outgrown and replaced a year earlier, which she always used for the same purpose; and they were ready.

'A nice little car,' Marie commented as Jane turned out of the byroad on to the B-road that descended into the town.

Jane considered it a horrid little car and she had every intention of changing it now that there was some money in the bank. She needed a 4x4 in the winter. '*Little* being the important word,' she said. 'I do a fair mileage around the farms . . . and the shoots. Fuel consumption's a major factor.'

'It will be the same for me when I can afford a private car, if there still are private cars if and when that day dawns. At the moment I can only manage a motor scooter.' For twenty miles they discussed the relative merits of the smaller cars. When they were halfway to Edinburgh, Marie said, 'You've been having an exciting time.'

'I've been having an exhausting time,' Jane replied. 'You knew that I was only married last month?'

'I could hardly not know it. Your picture was all over the papers. And on telly, but not the news. Did you know that you were the answer to a question on a quiz show?'

Jane tried very hard not to show surprise. 'No, I didn't,' she said. 'And don't tell me any more; I'm trying to forget the whole ghastly episode. When you get married, be sure to have a spare wedding dress hanging behind the door. And being recently married isn't why I'm exhausted, in case that's what you're thinking. I came back from my honeymoon to find that my locum had tackled all the easy work and left the rotten jobs for me to do. And then, on top, I find that I'm a witness again in the Knifeman case. I was his first victim and then I went and walked in on his fourth or fifth, I've lost count. All I need now is for a rock band to build a recording studio next door and keep me awake all night. Oh, and I'm pregnant, so I suppose that must add to the general exhaustion.'

Marie laughed. 'I'm told that it's tough at the top. And congratulations, by the way. You're looking very tidy,' she added with a quick glance at Jane's waistline.

'If you think this is the top, you're dreaming. And thank you, by the way . . .'

Traffic was almost non-existent at the early hour. They were in Edinburgh before eight a.m. Jane had Satnav for her work so they found the right house very easily. It was dark and silent; small and neat, slotted into a gap between larger houses in a street of prim respectability.

Jane tapped the Satnav. 'According to this, there's no back lane. If you ring the bell, I'll watch the back door, just in case.'

'Right.'

Jane followed a path to a rear corner of the house. She heard the bell ring. There were footsteps and then voices. She hurried round again to the front. Marie was confronting a woman in a dressing gown. 'This is Mrs Hemiston,' she told Jane. 'Cousin to Helen Maple. She tells me that Helen arrived here yesterday evening, cadged a meal, made a phone call and went away again.'

Mrs Hemiston was older than her cousin and less friendly. 'It's the truth. You can search the place if you want. I'm going back to bed. Some of us work for a living.'

'We both work for our livings,' Marie said. 'What number did she ring?'

'No idea.'

'Can I come in and use last number redial?'

'If you want. And a fat lot of good it'll do you. I forgot, she phoned for a taxi after that.'

'Which company?'

'City Cabs. Leastways, that was the number I gave her.'

'We may have to take you up on your offer to let us search,' Marie said tiredly. 'For the moment, go on back to bed.'

Jane and Marie withdrew to the car. Marie used her mobile phone to call Ian Fellowes. He had left strict instructions that he was not to be disturbed and the telephonist was more afraid of him than of Marie.

'I don't suppose he could get the address from City Cabs anyway,' Marie said.

'Leave this to me.' Producing her own mobile phone, Jane found that Honeypot's number was still programmed into it. She called the office and asked for Superintendent Potterton's extension. 'Tell her that Jane Highsmith is calling.'

After only a few seconds, Honeypot came on the line. 'Jane? How are you doing? But you're not Jane Highsmith now, are you? You're Jane Fox. I've been seeing your photograph in the papers.'

Jane ground her teeth. 'Will nobody ever allow me to forget the show that I made of myself? I was dealing with an injured puppy and it sprayed blood all over my wedding dress. Anyway, more to the point, I'm in Edinburgh just at the moment. Ian Fellowes invited me to find a witness who did a bunk so I'm here with one of his female officers. We were going to phone you as soon as we could count on you being at your desk.'

'In other words, you want help.' Honeypot was her usual perceptive self.

'You read me like a book. This girl we're after seems to have called on her cousin briefly and then phoned somebody else and called a taxi. We could hardly dash around your patch interrogating people,' Jane said in tones of virtue. She had her fingers crossed. 'And they probably wouldn't tell us anything anyway.'

'All right,' said Honeypot. 'You don't fool me for a moment, but I still owe you a favour. Give me all the relevant phone numbers and your own mobile numbers and I'll get somebody on to it straight away. I have a cadet who needs a little practice in kicking bums. Keep your phones switched on.'

They disconnected. Marie's eyes were popping. 'It's not what you know, it's who you know,' Jane said complacently. 'When she gets back to us, you can take over. Then some day you'll be able to remind her who you are. These contacts can count in your favour later.'

There was an open café on a street corner and they went in for a second breakfast. Then they went back and sat in the car. 'We ought to go back to Newton Lauder,' Marie said. 'These things take forever, especially at a weekend, and I'm sure Mr Fellowes has something useful for me to do.'

'You're probably doing something much more useful here,' Jane said. As she spoke her mobile phone played its little tune. She answered the call, stated the name of the café they were sitting outside, then smiled and expressed great enthusiasm and words of thanks before replacing the phone back in her handbag.

Marie swallowed nervously before asking what was going on. Jane smiled enigmatically but remained silent as she looked out of the car window.

A minute later she exclaimed, 'Ahhhh there she is,' before leaping out of the car and rushing over to a woman who was in the process of elegantly unfolding long, shapely legs out of a sleek, top-of-the-range Mercedes. 'Honeypot, how are you? So good of you to come in person,' Jane was saying to the very beautiful sophisticated woman who was now walking with Jane towards the car where Marie was sitting transfixed by the scene unfolding in front of her.

As they approached the little car, Marie forced herself

out of her paralysis and nervously came out of the car to greet them. Marie had to stop herself from curtsying as if she was meeting royalty, as the superintendent was after all the most important policewoman or policeman that Marie was ever likely to meet, let alone talk to.

'So sorry I couldn't make it to the wedding,' Honeypot was saying, 'but we had a rather important murder enquiry come up and I just couldn't get away. Read all about it though – and saw some photos. Nice dress,' she added with a teasing smile and a friendly punch of Jane's arm.

'Yes, yes, very funny,' Jane replied, before getting down to the business at hand as she'd really had enough teasing on that particular subject to last a lifetime – even from old friends she was asking favours of. 'So, any news on our disappearing witness?'

'Ahhh yes, back to the nitty gritty.' Honeypot almost looked disappointed having to get back to police work. 'Well, my hard-working cadet managed to find out for us that a certain Miss Maple took a taxi to the bus depot in St Andrews Square and caught the last coach to Aberdeen. We then found the coach driver – we were lucky, the driver had brought the same coach back to Edinburgh this morning and was about to go home. My wonderful cadet had managed to get hold of this photograph of your witness Helen Maple taken at your wedding, Jane.' Again, Honeypot had the beginnings of a teasing smile playing around her mouth as she showed them the photograph.

Jane was horrified to recognize herself in the background of the picture, skimpy dress and all.

'Anyway, our coach driver remembered Helen and, indeed, my cadet suspected that he had rather fancied her, which is wonderfully helpful as he then remembers her disembarking at the Kinross Services. And that, I'm afraid, is as far as my information goes.' Honeypot finished with a flourish, aware that she'd gone above the call of duty

– and probably friendship too – in taking so much time to pass on the information herself.

Jane told her as much when she thanked her again for coming to see her personally.

'Oh, it's nothing,' Honeypot replied. 'I had to see the blushing bride in person at some point, now didn't I? And to wish you another congratulations, I've just noticed . . .'

This time Jane didn't begrudge Honeypot her teasing smile and they embraced before saying a final goodbye.

Back in the car, Marie exhaled and exclaimed a mere, 'Wow!' She collected herself before adding, 'When Honeypot, sorry Superintendent Potterton, shook my hand goodbye she asked me if you'd told me about the well incident yet . . .? What does she mean?' Marie was genuinely confused, thinking there was some important fact that she was meant to have picked up about the case but failed to do so.

'Oh for goodness' sake,' Jane exclaimed, annoyed again by Honeypot's persistent teasing. 'When I was young my sister's boyfriend fell into a well. I was the only person small enough to be lowered down to attach a rope to him. Big deal!'

'Oh yes,' Marie said as recognition dawned. 'I remember the fuss on the tele now. It *was* a big deal.'

To change the subject, Jane brought them back to their current situation. 'I can do Kinross in an hour,' she said. 'Shall we go for it?'

'We'd be going off our patch. I'll speak to the DI.' Marie, back in work mode, made a call and this time was lucky and got through to Ian.

'You've done very well,' Ian said, 'with a little help from Honeypot. Yes, go to Kinross and then phone me again. I'll speak to Fife and make sure that it's all right.'

'Protocol, protocol,' Marie sighed as she put away her phone. The word sat oddly on her Highland lilt. 'Tell me more about going down the well.'

Jane raised her eyebrows and realized that as they were about to embark on a fairly long car journey her refusal to go into detail of that historic event would have to be rather short-lived if they were to have a remotely pleasant expedition.

SIXTEEN

Traffic remained light. Once they were clear of Edinburgh they devoured the motorway in good style and paused at Kinross Services for Marie to use the official credit card to fill Jane's tank. She then phoned Ian Fellowes again. Jane had two cups of coffee waiting. 'We're to wait here,' Marie said. 'Somebody from the Fifers will come and join us.'

They chatted over their coffee – not very good coffee as Jane remarked – and watched the traffic come and go. Most vehicles entering the services filled up with fuel and they had small bets as to which ones would park and come inside for a snack and, at long odds, which would be their contact. They had each been wrong several times when a man finally brought another coffee to their table. He was, he said, Detective Sergeant Lovelace. He was small for a policeman and old for a sergeant but he had a ready smile.

'How did you recognize us?' Marie asked.

'Lothian and Borders faxed a photograph through.'

'Head and shoulders, I hope,' said Jane. As far as she was aware there were very few recent photographs of her in circulation other than those from her recent wedding.

The sergeant produced his smile. 'The full monty,' he said. Jane's face felt hot. The sergeant sensed her discomfort and tactfully got back to the business at hand. 'It only took three phone calls. Your witness booked into a bed and breakfast in Kinross. But that landlady can't be doing with her overnighters hanging around all day, so by ten o'clock out they go and after six they can come back in again. Your witness probably has friends or relations in the town that she plans to spend the day with. Your best course of action would be to give us the facts and then get back to Newton Lauder and leave us to get a statement from her.'

Jane was getting tired of the sergeant who was revealing a rather patronizing manner. 'I'm afraid that wouldn't do,' she said. She seemed to be saying what everybody had been telling each other for days. 'The witness is very nervous and has already had a severe shock, which is why she upped and ran. I'm not police, but I was the first victim of Knifeman and I rescued her when she was the latest. She trusts me, so I was sent along for reassurance. There's something worrying her; we don't know what it is but she'll have to be coaxed, and not by strange cops.'

'I'm not really all that strange.' Lovelace tried to sound hurt. 'But point taken. If you follow me I'll point out the bed and breakfast and then you're on your own for the day. If you have a problem . . . Give me your mobile.'

He programmed his own number into Marie's mobile and led them into the car park. His car was a large but old Jaguar that they had noticed but dismissed on its arrival. They followed the big boot across the motorway and down into Kinross. The sun had come out and the old town was looking its best. The Jaguar paused outside a stone house with a glaring bed and breakfast sign at the gate while an arm emerged and pointed; then the big car accelerated away.

'I think we can trust them to have made sure that she isn't still hiding inside,' Marie said. 'Or might she have told the landlady a sob story?'

Jane weighed up her judgement of Helen's character. 'She might, but it's unlikely. If we go in asking questions we could do more harm than good. It's not a big town. Let's start looking in the sort of places where a single girl might pass the time.'

Three cafes and a souvenir shop later Jane said, 'Thar

she blows!' The expression might be unfamiliar to a Western Highlander so she added, 'There she is, in the red coat. We need somewhere private to talk so I'll fetch the car. You keep an eye on her.' She fetched the car from where it had been parked outside the Premier hotel. She could imagine returning to find both ladies vanished, but when she stopped at the kerb she received a nod and an upraised thumb from Marie, who was backed round from the shop door and leaning comfortably against a railing. Jane gave Marie the car keys and entered the shop.

Helen was browsing through a rack of magazines. When Jane tapped her arm she jumped and turned white. 'We need to talk,' Jane said. 'But not here. Come out.' Helen followed on rubber knees.

Marie had established herself in the front passenger seat of Jane's car. Jane and Helen settled in the cramped rear seats. Jane was well aware that she had only been sent along for reassurance but Marie seemed uncertain how to open the questioning, so Jane took charge.

'Why did you run away?' Jane asked.

Helen shook her head and pinched her lips together, then opened them to whisper, 'I can't tell you.'

That seemed to be a pretty comprehensive refusal to speak out. 'Can't or won't?' Jane asked.

'Both.'

Marie had produced one of the small recorders beloved of the modern, high-tech officer and stood it on the dashboard. She opened her mouth but closed it again without speaking. Jane had already slipped her own microwave reader out of a deep pocket, switched it on and swiped it over Helen's back. She also passed it over Marie's back for luck and then wondered what she would have done if it had registered positive.

Jane took a deep breath. 'Helen, I've dug you out of trouble once but I don't want to have to do it again. In fact, I *won't* do it again. I have things to do, a business to run and –' she remembered suddenly – 'a husband to look after. You're heading straight back into trouble but this time you're doing it on purpose and if that's the way you want it . . .'

Helen was shaking her head so that tears hopped down her cheeks. 'I never wanted any of this.'

Jane had to keep talking but she decided that her words were unimportant compared to a soothing tone of voice. 'But you're digging yourself deep into it. Can't you see what you're doing? I think I know for a fact that you're not Knifeman – never mind how I know – so you've got to be messing around on behalf of somebody else. Who is it? Relative? Boyfriend?' Helen's head-shaking was becoming frantic but Jane went on mercilessly. 'Can't you see how it's going to look? If a court doesn't think that you were Knifeman, probably with an accessory for days when you were known to be elsewhere, it will certainly believe that you're covering up for your nearest and dearest. When the police get hold of Knifeman, as they certainly will, the fact that you tried to avoid incriminating him or her will look very bad.' Jane was close to running out of arguments. 'Flight is evidence of guilt so by running away—'

To Jane's great relief, Helen broke down. 'I never wanted to be involved and I didn't want him to do it at all. We c-could have been happy as we were. I told him and told him that I couldn't do more for him than I was already doing even if we were set up together but he wanted us to be properly married with our own house, and he couldn't face the time it would take saving for a deposit as a first-time buyer. And it was all my fault because I said, joking, that if he'd give me that necklace out of the window I'd marry him straight away and he took me seriously and started picking up on the joke and saying that we could do it if he pretended to be Knifeman and I was horrified . . .' Helen paused to draw a deep, shuddering breath. 'I told him not to be so damn silly and I said that there was nowhere I could wear it if we came by it that way but he was talking less and less as if it was a joke and more as if it was a real plan. And then he walked into the shop with a knife and a length of clothesline and he said that he'd rather have me dead than walking around not his and he put the knife to my throat and made me lie down behind the counter.' Helen's voice was racked by distress but a note of pride was creeping in. It was not given to every woman to be so much desired . . .

'I think we know what came next,' Marie said, suddenly finding her voice. 'He left you tied up and you were angry because he didn't seem to care if you were stuck there until morning. So why are you trying so hard to protect him now?'

'Because . . .' Helen's voice died away.

'Because you still love him?' Jane suggested. Silence dragged slowly along.

Reluctantly, Helen nodded.

'Are you going to tell us who he is?' Jane persisted.

Helen shook her head.

'We can find out easily enough,' said Marie. 'We only have to ask around the town about who she has been keeping company with. Somebody who knows both of them will tell us.'

'At least it won't have been me,' Helen said. 'And I won't be confessing to being an accomplice.'

'There's no such thing or person as an accomplice in Scots law,' Marie said. 'Now, what became of the necklace? Does he still have it?'

Helen sat up straight. 'Would it make a difference if he was to give it back, voluntarily?'

'A big difference,' Jane said. 'Provided that he hadn't stolen anything else.' Once again she hoped she knew what she was talking about. It seemed logical and there was sometimes a streak of common sense threaded through the law. Not often but sometimes.

Helen produced her mobile phone. 'May I ring him?'
'Yes, of course.'

Helen kept the small screen out of Jane's view while
she selected a name and keyed for a connection. A male
voice answered. It took Jane a few seconds of visualizing
faces and testing the voice on them, but she identified it
at the third or fourth try. Helen quickly warned the other
that his identity would be known. 'Go and return that thing
to Mr Golspie,' she said, 'and they'll go easy on you. No,
not to the police, to Mr Golspie hisself. Apologize. Say
that you got carried away. Blame me if you like – say that
I pushed you into it. If you do that, I'll do whatever you
want but I'd most rather just get married even if it means
a council rental. Yes, I mean it. I promise.' She
disconnected.

'Who was the original Knifeman if you're saying your
man just copied him?' Marie asked suddenly.

Helen paled. 'Honest to God, I've no idea. If I knew,
I'd tell you.'

Jane got out of the car and took her seat behind the
steering wheel. 'We may as well be getting back to Newton
Lauder,' she said. 'Do we have to collect your overnight
things from the landlady?'

Helen feebly nodded her head and they set off. Perhaps
the reality of the situation was finally settling in around
her ears as she contemplated the part she'd played in the
stealing of the necklace. She just hoped that giving it back
would help matters, but she wasn't so sure . . .

SEVENTEEN

'Well, young lady,' said Ian Fellowes at his most paternal. 'You've led us quite a dance. We've asked around among the young people of the town and it seems that you have been seen in the company of more than one of the male contingent. Many more. From what Mrs Fox tells us you still have a special relationship with the young man who raided the jeweller's shop and left you tied up.'

'But he hadn't done any of the other thefts,' Helen said firmly. The air in Ian Fellowes's office seemed to be vibrating with discord. Marie remained there as of right, having escorted Helen there. Jane was still there because nobody had told her to get out and she was curious. DS Bright was taking a record as usual. The little room was packed.

'You don't know that for sure – how could you?'

'I could, because he was spending all his spare time with me. He talked about the robberies once or twice. Then he began to say that it would be a good idea to do something similar and let the other whoever-it-is take the blame so that we'd have the money to get married. Anyway, I'm not telling you who he is and I won't give evidence against him.'

'You realize that the law can force you to give evidence against him – you're not protected by marriage or anything – and more importantly he might attack again with more serious consequences?'

Helen shook her head so violently that her curls danced. 'I can make sure that he doesn't. He owed some money because he'd lost a bet and he wanted cnough to pay it, but I've been saving up and I can give him enough.'

'Bad move!' said Ian, looking very serious. 'Just let him get the idea that if he loses money gambling you'll make his losses good and he'll never stop. Never. It's happened over and over again.'

Helen's hands became fists. 'That's for me to worry about. As long as he keeps his nose clean it's no concern of yours.'

'It is very much a concern of mine as long as there's any likelihood of him trying it on again.'

'Which he wouldn't.'

'Which he certainly would. People get hurt that way. It's happened before. It happens all the time. Anyone can see it except for folk like you.' Ian pointed a finger into her face. 'He promises never to gamble again. He thinks he can win this time so breaks his promise. He loses. He can't bear to admit it to you. So he has another try at recouping his losses. And this time the victim tries to fight him off and serious blood gets spilled. So where does your boyfriend finish up?'

Helen got to her feet. 'I don't have to stay here and listen to this. You can't make me.'

'I could. Don't make me make you.'

'It's Alistair Ledbetter,' Jane said suddenly. For lack of seats she was standing with her back against the door.

Helen's knees gave way and she sat down with a thump on the hard chair. 'No!' she said. 'What's she doing here anyway? She's no right.'

Ian looked as though he had been on the point of saying the same, but he waved away the objection. 'You're sure?' he asked Jane.

'I'm afraid so,' Jane said. 'I was sure that the man I'd seen pass my window was somebody I knew and when . . . when you mentioned gambling losses I remembered Alistair trying to borrow money off me and insisting that his father mustn't know. I've been thinking it over and over and it would fit with my attack too. He could have had time to leave the limo behind the shops and get to my surgery in the time taken by Knifeman. And the same when I called him to pick me up. And I did think that his driving was a little shakier than usual.'

'But that doesn't prove anything,' Helen said desperately.

'No, of course it doesn't,' Ian said. 'But it tells us who to make enquiries about. When we start asking people whether you and young Ledbetter are a couple, what answer will we get?'

'They may say that we're a couple, but what does that prove? All right, Alistair tied me up. I'll complain to him all right but I'm not making any complaint to you and if you bring him into court I'll deny it. Perfectly loving couples do tie each other up sometimes.' She blushed scarlet. 'It's all part of the fun.'

'You didn't seem to be finding it fun when I found you,' Jane said.

'Either he has or he hasn't returned the necklace to Mr Golspie,' said Marie. She was standing beside Ian Fellowes. 'The mobile phone company can trace the call that she made. If that was to Alistair . . .' She broke off when Ian held up a restraining hand.

Ian picked up the phone. 'See if you can connect me with Mr Golspie the jeweller, either at home or in his shop.'

'All right,' Helen almost shouted. 'All bloody right. He did tie me up and pinch the necklace, all because I'd said something stupid. But I told him to give the necklace back, you heard what I said, and I hope he's done it by now or I'll be furious.'

'We'll find out, shall we?' Ian said.

'But do you still love him?' Marie asked. Ian looked at her curiously. Clearly Marie's question was, to her, the vital factor in the equation; but it should not weigh with an investigating officer.

Five minutes later they had the answer. Mr Golspie had

just returned to his shop and found a package on the floor below the letter box. It contained the missing necklace. There was no covering letter.

'There's an end to the matter, then,' Helen said.

'I'm afraid not,' said Ian. 'Bright, have Alistair Ledbetter fetched in here.'

Helen was aghast. 'But you can't do that. He's returned what he took.'

'Somebody seems to have returned what seems to be the stolen necklace,' Ian said, 'but none of that is proven. There's a strong presumption that whoever took one thing took others and is the Knifeman, but we can soon settle the matter. Miss – I'm sorry, Mrs Fox I should say. Do you have your microchip reader with you?'

Jane had become habituated to carrying her microchip reader in her roomy shoulder bag ready for just such a need. She placed it on the desk.

Ten sullen minutes later Alistair Ledbetter was brought into the room. The accompanying officer stood with his back to the door. Jane was pushed into a corner. Alistair looked at Helen with reproach in his eyes. His T-shirt was already loose at the back. At Ian's invitation he lifted it and Jane applied the reader. There was no reaction at all nor any sign of a scar or of metallic foil.

'Very well,' Ian said. 'It seems that you were not the robber of Miss Highsmith.' He snapped his fingers. 'I must get used to your new identity.'

'But at the time of the robbery I *was* Miss Highsmith,' Jane said, trying to keep amusement out of her voice. Alistair winked at her. He seemed to be in good spirits and confident of his own future.

'We still have a lot of enquiries to make,' Ian said. 'Do you have a passport?'

Alistair shook his head. 'Never needed one.'

'I'm releasing you on your own recognizances. A charge may or may not be brought later. Report to the desk downstairs once a day so that we always know where you are. If you have any information that could help to identify the real Knifeman, you would be doing yourself a favour by telling us.'

Alistair nodded and got to his feet.

'This evening,' Helen said quickly. He nodded again and left the room followed by his uniformed shadow.

Ian looked at DS Bright. 'See to the updating of the information on the boards in the incident room.' Bright nodded and made a note.

'You won't be needing me any more,' Jane said.

'Not for the moment. Unless you have any more useful ideas?'

'You'll be the second to know.' Ian looked blank. 'I'll be the first,' she pointed out. She left the building with a smile on her lips. Pulling Ian's leg had always been her favourite hobby.

EIGHTEEN

J ane found that she was living at a mad gallop. A new husband brought new demands for her attention and a growing baby bump brought its own challenges. They were in the process of selling the two houses that they had occupied as singles and so the ongoing services of Helen Maple (who Jane had insisted they should still keep employing despite the Knifeman investigation), which should have lightened the load, were largely taken up with cleaning and otherwise preparing the houses for sale. Jane's practice became overloaded when the only other vet within easy reach of the area was involved in an unsavoury scandal and lost half his clients. One of the experts who had authenticated the Raeburn painting changed his mind but his competence was called into question by other experts during a lawsuit over a different painting in different ownership – a lawsuit that seemed destined to last for ever.

All in all it was a relief to be summoned once more to Ian Fellowes's office where Jane could count on being allowed to think of only one thing at a time. She found the detective inspector leafing through a drift of statements and looking harassed. He got hurriedly to his feet and led her down to the former gymnasium.

The scene in what had become the incident room had suffered several changes, the most obvious of which was that the whiteboards now extended all around the room and were very largely covered with printing in many hands and colours; and dozens of photographs. Jane was relieved to note that her own wedding photographs were now almost completely obscured by later additions.

The collator was the only other person present. He, too, was looking harassed.

'I'll tell you the problem . . .' Ian said. He then fell silent.

Jane, who had spent much of the day so far on her feet, took a chair, put her feet up on another and let out a deep breath. The chairs, being police issue, were not noticeably more comfortable than tired feet but it made a change.

Ian found his voice. 'We've been going over and over the known facts and the reasonable suppositions about Knifeman. We've picked out everybody local who comes within a mile of conforming to the criteria of age, size, build and so on. We then deleted anyone who had a shatterproof alibi. We're left with twenty-two names of hot prospects. I'm hoping that you can help us to whittle down the list.'

'You have tested each of those with a microchip reader?'

'We have, but without a single positive result.'

'Then,' Jane said, 'your next step is to consult everybody who sells lead foil, especially those who advertise it on the Internet. That won't be conclusive, because aluminium foil is more effective than lead, but Knifeman doesn't necessarily know that. Or get each of your remaining suspects unexpectedly out of bed. I don't suppose Knifeman sleeps with aluminium foil taped over his left kidney.'

Ian brightened. 'Now, that's the sort of thinking I look to you for. You're sure that your two acquaintances are right and lead foil wouldn't do it? We've consulted several sources but the few who have so far replied disagree with each other.'

'It does it for X-rays. I have an old and very small X-ray machine because if an animal's brought in after a traffic accident I can't wait around for X-rays to come back from Edinburgh. The makers forced me to buy a lead apron and I had to promise to use it if I ever wanted to have babies, but I tried it out on X-ray film and aluminium foil worked better provided that you kept it uncrumpled.'

Ian eyed Jane's waistline, which was noticeably expanding. 'Are X-rays and microwaves the same?'

'I think they're more or less similar but on different wavelengths.'

Ian's eyebrows went up and up. *'Think? More or less? Similar?* That's not very positive.'

*'I'*m not very positive,' Jane said. 'You do rather spring these things on me at about ten seconds' notice; you never give me time to visit Google and I never did physics at school.'

'Well, don't get emotional about it. Mr Nicholson, please phone around the metal stockists, find out who's been enquiring about lead foil.' The collator nodded with dignity. 'But first find out about microwaves and lead foil. Ask Forensics again or try the universities. Somebody must know. Now, Jane, what I really brought you here for . . . You grew up here, went to school with most of your generation and to judge from your wedding wingding you're very popular. I want you to go through the list of probables with me and tell me what you know about them. The clues must be somewhere.'

'All right. Go ahead.'

Nicholson drew the blinds, producing an almost ecclesiastical dimness. A square of whiteboard had been kept free of writing and of photographs and here Ian focused a projector. 'Suspect Number One,' he said. 'Rupert Williamson. These are in no particular order.'

'Definitely not if he's first in line,' Jane said. The young man whose image flashed on to the screen had the face of a conceited bulldog. 'You must have put him on the spot, questioning him. He has no need of money—'

'That is not what our man was told by the boy's father.'

'Probably not. The father thinks the boy should learn the value of money so he keeps him on a tight rein. The mother has money of her own and what Rupert wants Rupert gets.'

The photograph was evidently stored in the computer. A row of symbols ran down the right-hand margin. One of the symbols vanished.

'Next,' Ian said. 'His brother Quentin. We included him because we could see no way that he could afford to run around in a nearly new Morgan. We didn't know that he had a rich and indulgent mum.'

'And now you know. There will be more the same.' Jane paused for thought. 'Did you hear the story of the priest in the Highlands who told his flock all about hell and how they would burn forever in the fiery furnaces. "Lord," said the flock, "we didna ken." And the Lord in his infinite maircy and wisdom looked doon from above and said, "Weel, ye ken fine noo."' Telling an ancient story had given Jane time to think and she had decided that it was time to reveal a delicate secret. 'You may as well know that when we were young Quentin and I had a thing going. And, Ian, I would prefer that Roland never knew about this.'

'I quite understand,' Ian said. 'Did you . . . were you . . .?'

'That,' Jane said sternly, 'is none of your damn business, copper or not. Whatever you need to know, if I know it you will too; but it's thus far and no further, no matter how your salacious curiosity drives you on. Quentin was – probably still is – a rather intense young man. What he wants he wants urgently and desperately, and that would usually get through to fond Mum, who coughed up in the end. Much the same probably applies to Rupert.' Jane paused. 'Usually.'

'But?'

'Yes, there's a but. Fond Mum loves both sons to the point of folly but she is a religious and very moral person. Anything that she thinks might be intended for the pursuit of girls of whom she might not approve, especially as prospective daughters-in-law, that they do not get. I remember an occasion when Quentin wanted to take me

to the races at Kelso and Mum was thoroughly in favour.'
Jane flushed delicately pink. 'But when he wanted to book
rooms for us nearby rather than drive home overnight, that
was quite different. Never mind that he showed her the
confirmations of bookings at two different hotels half a
mile apart, from that moment I was, to her, an immoral
slut only after her son for money and sex. Who's next?'

'Alex McCall.'

'That's a terrible photograph; he's much better-looking
than that. He has an alibi that he'll produce if you push
him hard enough. He's having an affair with a married
lady. This,' Jane said sadly, 'is another category that may
turn up more than once. Bored and neglected housewife,
bored and randy youth, spare bedroom at one house or the
other or, if both houses are seriously overlooked, the Canal
Bar has a room upstairs that can be rented by the hour,
possibly by the minute for all I'd know. I regret having to
mention it because if you forbid the practice where will
the young ones go in cold weather?'

Ian looked at her, pop-eyed. It seemed that his view of
the denizens of his territory was suffering a change. 'If
nobody makes a complaint we won't interfere. Number
Four. June Pherson, the first of the girls.' The screen showed
a well-built young lady in jeans and a T-shirt, treating the
camera to a come-on smile.

'A possibility,' Jane said. 'I was at school with her. She
never did have much of a bosom and her voice is gruff. She's
been saving up to buy a car, for what purpose I wouldn't
care to guess but she was always one for the boys. I don't
know how far she's got with the car but she's not very bright
and the best job she could get pays about tuppence a year.'

'Five and six, the brothers Dick and Angus Plum. The
way the alibis worked out it could only be one of them if
they were in league.'

'Very unlikely. They don't get on. And Angus could do
it but Dick's the original model for the cowardly lion.

He can talk tough but if somebody stands up to him he'll cave in.'

'Is there anyone else who could be Angus Plum's accomplice?'

'And give him a false alibi? I doubt it. He's an arrogant sod and universally disliked. You should look very hard at anyone bearing witness for him and if it's his mother he's guilty.'

'Hmm. Seven, Bruce Dalgrain.'

'I can't see him in the part. He's vain, always dapper. I can't visualize him in a spotty T-shirt or old trainers. That's a personal opinion. I suppose criminals often adopt disguises that are out of character for them – that's what a disguise is for, after all – but Bruce is too concerned with his image. I suppose,' Jane said slowly, 'there comes a point beyond which he won't stoop. More certainly,' she picked up speed again, 'most of the descriptions so far, including the one I gave you, were of a young person who would only have to snatch off a baseball cap or change his shoes to melt into the background, but Bruce would never do any melting. His mother can hardly afford any of it, she takes in mending to make ends meet, but Bruce loves his gold watch and having his hair styled every week and . . . and . . .'

'Don't go on,' Ian said. 'You've made your point. Eight, next girl. Joyce Stiggs.'

Jane had to think for a moment. 'It's only an impression but I think Joyce is taller than Knifeman. Not by much and, of course, I've always seen Joyce in shoes with heels. Her mother must be earning very good money but I don't know how much of that reaches Joyce. However, Joyce does have her own job with Lance Kemnay, so she is earning. And, if Helen Maple isn't available, Joyce takes over my surgery for me sometimes, just selling dogmeal, toys and non-prescription medicines when I'm out on the farms, and she seems honest. I don't know what she'd especially want money for. She's the type of girl who expects a man to pick up the bill every time. She's one who would certainly know about the steel box, but no, I'm not convinced – she's too moral in that sort of self-congratulatory way to do something like this.'

'Nine. Alistair Ledbetter.'

'Ah. Physically, he's a good fit. You asked me once whether he'd have had time and, thinking it over, yes, I think he would. He tried to borrow money from me on my wedding morning, would you believe? He chases girls and I know he gambles sometimes; for either hobby, you can need more money than I could expect him to make as a driver and odd-job man. And we now know, of course, that he and Helen carried out a copycat burglary at the jeweller's. I'm still not convinced that he's innocent of the other burglaries considering his figure fits my profile . . .'

'That seems reasonable. Ten, Barry Jenkins.'

'A bit of a nonentity. He works as a quantity surveyor and he's still struggling to get qualified. I honestly wouldn't expect him to have enough get-up-and-go to embark on a crime without being led into it. He's saddled himself with a St Bernard bitch that must eat him out of house and home – he never seems to grudge her better steaks than he buys for himself. And soft toys that she usually rips to bits. She's always ailing with some feminine trouble or another or else he imagines that she is, and then he has her down to me in about two jumps. He pays his bills promptly, I'll say that for him.'

'Eleven. Hugh Dodd.'

'But he was a victim!'

'Not with his own money. Whenever you get a series with a mystery figure lurking in the background the culprit has usually included himself as a victim, thinking to divert suspicion.'

'Oh. I hadn't thought of him that way. I don't know a lot about him – he's one of those people who just are.

They turn up behind counters and vanish again. He's always been polite, moderately competent, admires good cars and motorbikes without ever having shown signs of wanting to own one. I believe he's quite a good mechanic but too lazy to study the subject. I think his head's the right shape.'

Ian nodded, still writing. 'Twelve. James Haddon.'

'I wondered when you'd come to him. You must have got all this from other sources but yes, he's about the right build and yes, he needs money. He was caught with his hand in the till at the supermarket. He got off with a suspended sentence so it made other employers wary. Some of us have been trying to give him another chance. I let him come up, do some gardening and wash the car now and again, but as long as he's generally considered unemployable he just can't get the experience to be useful at anything in particular. Couldn't you get him taken on by the fuzz?'

'With a criminal record? In theory such things can be arranged; in practice I'd have to recommend him and my head would be on the block if he proved to be a recidivist.'

'But—'

'Have you given him a reference for some other job?'

'Well, no.'

'There you are, then. Send him for a job interview with your own recommendation and, even if he doesn't get it, I'll consider him. Or wouldn't he be a perfect candidate for Kempfield? You should recommend him in your position as one of the governors. Now, enough about him, on to number thirteen, Gemma Bristow.'

Jane turned her attention away from James Haddon but the subject was not closed permanently. 'Gemma fits physically, she can put on a gruff voice when she wishes and she's a competent actress with the local drama group; but she's compulsively honest. If she finds a coin or a glove in the street she'll come trotting in here with it.'

'Character can change suddenly, given temptation or a

trauma,' Ian said, 'but I'll note what you say. Fourteen, Helen Maple.'

Jane frowned. 'I'm not sure what to say about Helen. Always very fit – she used to go rock-climbing with a group of boys. She's never been half-hearted about anything – if she wants something she'll go for it. She has a rusty old motor scooter but she does sometimes borrow a friend's pushbike when her scooter's broken down. She doesn't fit in with any group but she always seems frank and open.'

'So do all the best con artists,' said Ian. 'Last one. Ewan Foster.'

Jane threw up her hands. 'What idiot put him on the list? He's got a *limp*, for God's sake!'

'I was waiting for your input,' Ian said weakly. 'The interviewing officer thought he was putting it on.'

'Then he's been putting it on ever since he had polio as a child. One question. Have you visited the local bookie, whatever his name is, to find out who's been losing money?'

'Yes, of course. But we don't have a resident local bookie. Most of the bets are placed by phone or email; nobody's name came up who we've been discussing, except for young Ledbetter.'

'I'm glad. Have you finished with me for now? I don't think I've been any help.'

'You've probably been lots of help,' Ian said, 'but I won't know for sure until we've chewed and digested what you've given us.'

'And you'll remember . . .?' Jane prompted anxiously.

'I shan't go rushing to Roland to ask whether he knew that his bride had had a schooldays romance – as who didn't? I'm not in the business of wrecking marriages. In fact, you'd be amazed at the lengths we sometimes go to in order not to damage a possibly salvageable marriage. I hope you never find out the hard way.'

'There's little danger of that,' Jane said, but below the level of her knee her fingers were crossed.

NINETEEN

For the week following Jane's attempt to filter a little light into Ian's list of possible Knifemen she was conscious of a mental itch – an idea, not leading towards an individual's identity but towards a general area in which this might be found. It was too elusive to be offered to Ian or his team, sometimes coming near the daylight to show itself in one form and then fading again into the shadows to approach once more in a different guise.

The Friday of that week came in dark and muggy; the sun peeped down through the clouds several times but never for more than a nervous blink, yet the events of that day acted like the much needed ray of sunlight, shining into Jane's tangled thoughts to put a focus where it was needed. The working part of the day had dragged past with the usual few cases of genuine need and the many cases of careless ownership or unnecessary panic.

The last case of the afternoon had featured a mastiff with a false pregnancy and a nervous owner – a combination that she had barely managed to dismiss with the aid of some reassuring words and a placebo. The mastiff had made up her mind that she would have her non-existent pups in a corner of Jane's surgery and the bitch was rather larger and considerably stronger than her mistress. Jane's back had been troubling her since lifting an overweight Labrador on to the table that morning and she had no intention of risking aggravating any injury – or endangering her pregnancy – by joining in the tug-of-war, so a serious stalemate was imminent until a convenient passer-by added his strength to that of the owner and fairly dragged the huge dog out to the owner's car.

Jane was relieved and grateful but much less so when she realized that the passer-by had no intention of passing but was coming into the surgery. He was, in fact, Ossy Hepworth, one of the very last people she would have welcomed. He took a cautious look around the surgery and then beckoned to somebody out in the Square. Bart slipped in as quickly as he could, considering the weight of his wrapped bundle.

Jane came within a micron of blowing her top. 'I've told you and told you,' she said. 'No more. None. Not one. Never. Not ever. Put it out of your mind.'

'You wouldn't leave a dog to suffer,' Bart said. The argument between them was so old that he did not even attempt to sound persuasive.

Out of love for all dogs – some breeds more than others – Jane had conceived an overpowering hatred of dogfighting. The instinct to fight, to defend family or territory or the right to mate, still lingered strongly in most breeds but the idea of putting a pair of aggressive dogs to fight it out was abhorrent to her. For once, as with the dead lion in the Bible story, it seemed that good might come from evil.

Her thoughts turned to her last visit to the seaside, some years earlier, where Jane had inserted a coin into a telescope on the front. This had allowed the viewer to turn a handle that focused the telescope. The resulting view had been disappointing except for the pleasure of observing the activities of people who thought themselves unobserved. While she pondered on this memory, she almost heard again the metallic rattle of the falling coin. Her idea was coming into focus, becoming sharper by the second.

'This really is the last time,' said Bart. He seemed surprised to find that he was speaking truth for once and

his voice found a fresh conviction. 'I'm retiring. Owning
the dogs is a mug's game. You're just getting fond of
them, and they come to trust you, and then they get
damaged, worse even than a clever and sexy young vet
can put together again, and you have to put them down
and you get to know what they mean by *heartbreak*.
Thanks be, I've got another line of business.' He had
manoeuvred Jane against her surgical table and while he
spoke he was uncovering a bull terrier with a badly bitten
face.

'It's going to happen again,' Jane said. 'I can't save this
eye. Can a one-eyed dog still . . . perform?'

'I said I was giving up owning fighting dogs. You want
to listen, lassie. I'm going to keep this one for a pet. One
good eye will be enough.'

Jane's idea burst like a plant into full flower. 'And of
course you'll need a guard dog, carrying that money around
when you're a bookie.'

Bart jumped as though prodded with a pin. 'Who said
anything . . .?'

Jane still had her surgical gloves on. She prepared and
administered an anaesthetic injection. The dog, which
had been trying to lick Bart's hand, closed its eyes and
relaxed into sleep.

'Here, what did you do to him?' Bart demanded in a
voice that rose into a squeak.

'Put him to sleep. No, not for keeps; but you needn't
think I'm going to approach the biting end of an awake
and wounded Staffy with surgical instruments in my hand.
I'm not that daft.'

'He wouldn't've touched you. Gentle as a lamb, he is.'

'And that's how she got those wounds to her head?'
There was no reply from either of the brothers. 'There
are scars of old cat scratches, so you've been training her
to fight. And now you're going to be a bookie full-time,
are you?' Jane knew that the training of dogs to fight

begins with pitting them against cats. She was already
cleaning and disinfecting the wounds. Lucrezia had been
lucky. Her eye was past saving but the bones of her face
were unbroken and the flaps of skin were still there. Only
cleaning and needlework was called for. 'Will you have
a monopoly or does anybody else make a book at the
dogfights?'

'They better bloody not,' said Ossy.

'Well, what I want from you is to know who's been
losing money heavily. There's always one damn fool who
goes on increasing his bets to try and win back his losses.
Who have you been leaning on to pay up?'

'Here!' Seeing Ossy under the bright lights she noticed
for the first time the scarring on his face and the once-
broken nose. Evidently Ossy was the enforcer of the part-
nership. He leaned forward and scowled into her face. 'You
can't expect that sort of info.'

Jane did not take kindly to menace. She had a large
scalpel in her hand and she let them see it. Each took a
step back. 'That sort of info is exactly what I expect and
if I don't get it . . . just remember that I know all the
animal people around here and most of them owe me a
favour or two, just like you do. Well, I'm calling in my
favours and if I'm not satisfied I'll be tipping off the police
and the SSPCA when and where the next dogfight's going
to happen. And I may not be too secretive about who let
the cat out of the bag. That won't make you popular with
the followers of illegal dogfighting. On the other hand, if
you help me now you'll be helping the police. I won't
even say where the information came from until the next
time you're in trouble. Then I'll tell them that you provided
the information that enabled them to put away the
Knifeman.'

The two brothers locked eyes, apparently conferring
telepathically. 'Is that who you're after? We'll do it,' Bart
said suddenly, 'if you'll not charge us for fixing up

Lucrezia there.' He nodded at the bloodstained bundle on the table.

'You've got a bloody nerve,' Jane said, 'but it'll be worth it if it gets you off my back for ever. Just don't ever tell anyone who takes over supplying the dogs that he can bring them to me when they get their bits chewed off.'

An hour later, when the brothers had carried the limp bundle out to their van, Jane was on the phone to Ian Fellowes before even beginning the clean-up of the surgery. She gave him a truncated and bowdlerized version of the story of her dealings with the brothers Hepworth. Ian could quite see that this was not a matter to be discussed on a landline phone.

'Stop there,' he commanded. 'I'm coming over.'

He was in Jane's surgery within ten minutes, unaccompanied. The preliminary courtesies took less than fifteen seconds.

'The way I see it,' Jane said, 'is that Knifeman may be driven to it by debt, probably a big gambling debt. You've already checked the legitimate bookies, or so you say, but you can't get to those who take bets on illegal activities; and the only one of those illegal activities to thrive around here is dogfighting, or if there are any others they don't come to the attention of a local vet. Reluctantly, I've let myself be pressurized into patching up injured dogs. I'm guessing that the brothers have been leaning on somebody who has been losing money to them and that that somebody may have been Knifeman acting out of fear or to keep his or her bad habits out of the ken of a strict parent or partner. They'd be prepared to let you know who the big losers have been, but that would mean admitting to you that they participate in – and probably promote – dogfighting. And I'm not going to get the list for you because that might mean admitting to the SSPCA that I'd been aiding and abetting.'

Ian looked at her, stone-faced. 'I'm trying very hard,'

he said at last, 'to forget what you tell me as fast as I hear it. If it ever got out that I'd turned a blind eye to dogfighting my time in the police would be done.'

'But if I just brought you the list . . .? I could say that it had only just been brought to me. Could you keep the SSPCA off my neck if the poo hits the fan?'

'I think so. If I get hold of the right senior man beforehand and say that the facts had just reached me anonymously.'

'But I can't give you dates and places of the dogfights in advance,' Jane said. 'And you needn't look as though I've just stolen your lollipop. You must see that I can't. They won't cough up any information unless I promise not to spill all the beans.'

'And your promise is binding even if it permits the severe wounding of dogs?'

It was a potent argument. Jane did indeed consider her promises binding. She fell silent. 'There is a way around it,' she said at last. 'Let's suppose that I get them into a suitably malleable frame of mind and then leave you to make the promises.'

'Here!' said Ian and, 'Hey! I can't afford to get it put around that my promises aren't to be trusted. All my sources would dry up immediately.'

'How terrible for you!' Jane said. They were still in her outer surgery and she was leaning, as usual, across the counter while Ian sat in the client's chair.

She relaxed and waited. Ian could be remarkably devious for a Lowlander at times. He did not disappoint her. Sometimes she thought that there must have figured a Highlander among his ancestors. 'There's a sergeant in Traffic,' he said, 'who is due to retire next month. His mate got knifed in Dundee and nearly died, so he hates knife crime. You get me the list without making any promises and introduce him to a suitably indiscreet member of the doggy fraternity and he can spill the beans in his own time.'

'And I don't have to break any promises,' Jane said, 'you keep your reputation for trustworthiness and with a little luck it puts an end to dogfighting around here.' *For a month or two*, she added silently. She knew that it would take a nuclear holocaust to stamp out dogfighting for ever.

TWENTY

Sergeant Midmill was, as promised by Ian Fellowes, on the verge of retirement, but he still had a full head of curly brown hair only slightly greying and his face was unlined. He had a ready and charming smile but he exhibited the promised hatred of knife crime and fell in willingly with the plan to entrap Knifeman.

Two weeks slipped away before the two Hepworth brothers could or would make themselves available for a conference at a time that suited Jane's plans. They were understandably suspicious but less so than might have been expected. Jane's word was known to be her bond; less well known was the conflict in train between that bond and the combination of her hatred of dogfighting and her grudge against Knifeman. During that period Jane had managed to speak in secret with a scrap metal dealer and three separate farmers in order to discover the information this part of the investigation desperately needed to reach a bargaining point with the two Hepworth brothers. Jane had had to work hard at prising the information out of the scrap metal dealer; however, the farmers in particular were easily brought to heel. Today's farmer is so hedged around with regulations and restrictions that he will almost inevitably stray occasionally over the strict boundaries set by the Law; and nobody is better placed to observe these deviations from strict compliance than the local vet.

For once, the brothers arrived in Jane's surgery without lugging between them a bloodstained and whimpering bundle. 'What's this about?' asked Bart.

Jane thought that his manner was already defensive. She was in no mood to tiptoe around the subject. She gave him a look that might well have burned a pair of holes in his hide. 'I think you can well guess what it's about,' she said. 'It's about tomorrow afternoon's scheduled dogfighting meeting at Prospect Wood, which is between Harrow and North Yielding Farms. I want that list of punters who owed you money last month and the month before and also who has paid off that debt or a substantial part of it. I personally don't want that information and I'd rather not know, but if you don't cough it up to Sergeant Midmill, who is waiting to come and have a word with you, the police, the SSPCA and the landowner will be informed of the planned dogfighting and word will be spread that you were the source of the leak. And you needn't bother looking daggers at the place where you quite wrongly believe my heart to be,' she added bravely. 'On this subject I don't have one and anyway my husband's video camera is watching and listening, linked to a recorder in the police station. Here's pencils and paper.'

The bluff worked. The violence that had seemed imminent faded away. Ossy began to write.

'One name stands out,' Ian said later back at the police station when the brothers had sulkily handed over the list and retreated back home. 'Well, I already had my suspicions about young Ledbetter, but not this one. Each of the others had paid off his or her debt or has a shatterproof alibi for most of the days in question, including Ledbetter. This one really has the gambling bug – their name doesn't pop up among the clients at the betting shop, so presumably they prefer the illegal kind of gambling rather than the more tame version, probably so no one knows about it – and any pretence of an alibi is the kind of waffle that a first-year police cadet could spit through the holes in without touching the sides.'

Jane chuckled at the idiom while regretting the identity of the suspect. 'I'm afraid so,' she said. 'But I wouldn't mind being a fly on the wall during that interview.'

'Maybe that could be arranged,' Ian said. 'I can certainly see possible advantages in having you on hand. I'll phone you.'

He came on the phone two days later and invited Jane to attend at the police station. The local animals had entered a period of health and the inoculations were as near up to date as they ever come, so that Jane was free to accept the invitation. DS Bright escorted her to Ian Fellowes who took her under his wing and led her to a very small, dull and bare-looking room on the ground floor. This was furnished only with a half-dozen folding chairs. The single small window looked into another, larger room, the typical interview room with more chairs, a table and some audio-visual equipment.

Ian indicated the window. 'So-called one-way glass,' he said. 'Pull up a chair.'

Jane pulled up a chair. 'I've heard of this but when I've seen it on the telly I've assumed that it was a camera trick. I never believed that glass could be made that could only be looked through from one side.'

'And you were right. This is only mirror glass, so thinly silvered as to be transparent. The result is that you can see from the dark side to the brighter lit side and not the other way round.' He touched a switch beside the door, which was well within his reach in the tiny room; the lights dimmed and the window became a mirror. He lowered the light level again and it was a window. 'From that side, we're invisible just now,' he said, 'but do remember that it is not soundproofed. If you speak above a murmur you'll give the game away.'

'I'm disappointed. It's like being shown how a simple conjuring trick works.'

'And I thought I was doing you a favour!' Ian said. 'I may as well tell you now that there may be rather more drama than you expect. There has been another and more serious incident and I'm only letting you witness this interview so that you can make a positive identification of the culprit, sufficient to allow us to make an immediate arrest. You're one person who has heard Knifeman's voice and seen how he moves.'

Jane felt her insides swoop downwards. 'What's happened? Who to?'

'I may as well tell you,' Ian said. 'You'll hear in a minute or two anyway. One of our staff, a telephonist, was on a day off. She's been in the habit of visiting a neighbour to do his errands for him. She was due to collect his prescriptions from him and collect his medications from the pharmacy but she got no answer at his door. She was wondering what to do when she noticed a few blood spots on the doorstep. That was enough. Remembering a talk I'd had with her she called the emergency switchboard. Bright attended. Using his initiative correctly for once, he broke glass and entered. He found the householder stabbed and dying. He died in the ambulance without speaking.'

'I'm not the only—'

Ian hushed her. The interview room was becoming occupied. Marie Webb brought Helen Maple in and then took up a position with her back against the door. They were joined by Sergeant Midmill who, with a show of consideration, made Helen as comfortable as the austere room permitted. Helen was looking unusually smart in a brown linen dress printed with a faint pattern of flowers; and, matching the colour of the dress, polished fashionable knee-high boots.

Midmill went through the ritual of telling the recording devices who was present and when. 'About the assault on you by Knifeman . . .' he began.

Helen gave a hiss of indrawn breath in protest. 'That wasn't the real Knifeman,' she said. 'That was only Alistair Ledbetter trying it on as a once-in-a-lifetime thing.'

'I'm sure you hope so. Do you think he knows the identity of the real Knifeman?'

Helen seemed to be caught flat-footed. She looked in Sergeant Midmill's direction but her eyes were not focused on him. Helen thought that they were looking into the distance. After a few seconds that seemed to add up to a full minute she said, 'You're trying to trap one of us or even both.'

Midmill chuckled. 'No point trying to pull the wool over your eyes,' he said. 'I'll ask again, quite openly. Do you think that your boyfriend knows who the real Knifeman is?'

'No, I'm sure he doesn't.'

'What makes you so sure of that?'

Once again it took Helen several seconds to formulate a reply. 'If he knew, he'd have told me.'

'Why?'

'Why? Just in the course of general conversation.'

'You discussed the identity of Knifeman?'

'Yes, of course. So did half the town, maybe more than half.'

'And he never dropped a hint as to who Knifeman might be?'

'No.'

'And nor did you?'

'How would I? I have no idea who Knifeman is.' Helen was beginning to sound out of breath.

'That surprises me. When you pretended to have been assaulted by Knifeman, you imitated and described him. I'm told that you're a prominent member of the Amateur Dramatic Society, and a skilled one.'

'I can't help what you've been told. And I never imitated him. I just described what I'd heard. And I don't think I was very accurate or very detailed, I just said that he was a little taller than I am.'

'So you did,' said Midmill. 'So you did. And you said that his shoes were black and highly polished.'

'I don't think I said quite that. I probably said that they were of black leather but in need of a clean.'

'Like his bicycle?'

'I never saw his bike.'

Midmill did not look in the least put out. 'Didn't you also comment that his head was shaped like a chimney pot?'

Jane leaned close to Ian Fellowes. 'It wasn't Helen who told you that—'

'Ssh!' Ian frowned and put a finger to his lips. 'He's trying to catch her out.'

'Not very subtly.'

Back in the interview room, Helen was beginning to look a little ruffled. 'I'm sure I didn't say that. Nobody ever asked me about the shape of his head,' said Helen, 'but that might have been a fair description.'

'Come now, Miss Maple,' said Midmill. 'You have said quite enough, and in what you have said your references to Knifeman universally point away from yourself – and away from Alistair Ledbetter. That might well be described as a giveaway. Anybody with a bad conscience trying to transfer suspicion to somebody else will usually try hard to make sure that the description is of somebody wholly unlike themselves. Please allow Miss Webb to pass her hand down your back. There may be occasion later for a body search.' Perhaps this time a full body search would show the foil that she'd been using to cover up the microchip.

Helen Maple jumped to her feet. 'I don't know what you're after . . .'

'I'm after the outline of a sheet of metal foil,' said Midmill.

'But you've no right to intrude on my privacy like this.'

'Miss Maple, I assure you that we have every right, but if you continue to raise objections you may force me to go ahead and charge you. I believe that you have been guilty of armed robbery—'

'I wish to use the toilet,' Helen said excitedly. 'I have the right and you can't stop me. Any court—'

'Constable Webb will accompany you.' Sergeant Midmill leaned across the table to switch off the recorder as Marie Webb collected together a sheath of papers from the table. She took her time in sliding back her chair and getting ready to escort Helen from the interview room.

At this point, Ian Fellowes leaned in close to Jane. 'He'll bring her to my room afterwards,' he said, 'and it might be neater if we were to get there first. Come on.'

Both groups were now rising to their feet. Ian Fellowes, preoccupied with proceedings still to come, acted in accordance with ingrained habit. He reached across to switch off the light. The switch, however, had three positions and had been in the middle or low setting, between 'off' and 'bright'. With the sudden decrease in the light level, the window became a mirror again and the interview room was invisible to both Jane and Fellowes.

TWENTY-ONE

For what took place next in the interview room and elsewhere Jane had to rely on fragments of talk and
extracts from evidence given months later in court.
Ian Fellowes would not have made his disastrous mistake
with the light switch if he had not been distracted by
worrying how Helen's words might slot into the wider
picture. For the same reason he was slow to see his error
and to dim the light again in what might well be termed
the *cabinet de voyeur*. The result was that Helen was given
several seconds to see and understand the apparently
magical transformation of the mirror into a window. By
the time the explanation had dawned on her, Ian had moved
the switch again and the view was gone. Jane heard a riot
of sound that Marie Webb later interpreted for her.

'I never saw such a change in a person,' Marie said.
'One moment she was as sweet as sugar, butter wouldn't
melt, you'd hardly believe it, the next a look came over
her face and it was as if she'd been taken over by a devil.
It made a shiver run up my back. Fury doesn't begin to
describe it.' The policewoman's eyes were wide. She was
being transformed into a superstitious islander. 'And she
was beginning a rant. I could hardly make out a word of
it except for "traitress", which came into it again and
again. I recognized your name more than once and I did
not like the tone at all. I hope nobody ever speaks of me
like that. I could see that she was ready to be violent so
I fetched out the handcuffs. But she was quicker. You
saw those knee-high boots she was wearing, looser than
riding boots but not as loose as gumboots? She made one
snatch. There was a loop of thin twine, the same colour

as the boot and almost invisible, which is why I never saw it, and out of the top of her right boot she came up with that kitchen knife the victims described. I tried to get between her and the door – Mr Fellowes says I was mad to do any such thing – but she slashed at me with the knife. I ducked my head quickly or she'd have cut my throat, and as it was she nearly scalped me. I'd no idea that the top of the head could bleed so much and I've been in and out of surgery while they trace each source of bleeding. They suture one cut and another starts to bleed. I've more stitches in my scalp than a wedding dress.'

Jane was visiting Marie in the local hospital – they could see Ian's window from where they sat. The town looked too peaceful to have hosted any such carrying on. Marie was bandaged almost beyond recognition. 'Well, I think you were very brave,' Jane said.

'Mr Fellowes said that I was as daft as you were when you went down that well. I didn't feel a bit brave, I just knew that if I stood aside and let her run past me I'd be doing the wrong thing and then I would be mad – mad at myself! I had some training in Unarmed Combat and how to disarm a person who's coming at you with a knife, but it doesn't seem to work if the other person has a real knife and means to fillet you like a herring.' Marie's soft voice with its Highland lilt died away leaving Jane to wonder whether the other really meant what she said.

Ian Fellowes gave his evidence in the later trial more fully but less colloquially than what he said to Jane, which essentially was: 'I got out of there and into the corridor damn quick and there she was just coming out of the other door with that evil-looking knife in her hand and dripping blood. But I suppose it only looked evil in hindsight – at the time it was just a bloodied kitchen knife. I could only assume that she'd killed Marie Webb. I was all set to be just as big an idiot as she was – Marie Webb, I mean, not the Maple girl – and I did just as I'd been taught at Hendon quite a long time ago, but I fumbled it and the knife went through between my hands and got me –' Ian paused and rubbed the shoulder of the arm in a sling – 'damn close to that major artery they call the carotid or the jugular, I can never remember which is which. I went down with the shock of it. I thought she was going to stoop and cut my throat and I was ready to kick her through the ceiling if I could, but she changed her mind, maybe she sussed out my intention. She ducked out of the interview room and ran for the emergency fire doors. I was in no doubt that she'd flipped her lid . . .'

The sergeant on the desk had his own story to tell and his own more northern dialect to tell it in. 'Yon quinie cam oot o the emergency ootgang wi her gullie a' bluidie. A thocht it maun be another damn test or a training exercise. Afore a jaloused a shid stap her, she was oot an awa.'

Behind the police station is an area of tarmac, divided up for the use of visitors, the parking of police cars, the depositing of cars seized from motorists who have overstepped the mark, badly damaged police cars awaiting treatment in the adjoining garages and sundry other purposes. Among these vehicles was a scattering of officers going on or coming off duty, collecting or parking police cars or sneaking out of the offices for a secret smoke. The sudden arrival of a bloodstained and crazy-looking young woman with her hair flying, brandishing an equally bloodstained knife, fell so far outside the experience and instructions of these officers that one and all waited for a lead that was not forthcoming until Ian Fellowes burst out of the building spouting blood and calling for first aid and the immediate arrest of the woman. But by then she had rounded the corner of the hotel and vanished into the wood beyond and moments later Ian fainted from loss of blood.

Inside the building a more orderly scene soon prevailed.

Jane, drawing on her medical experience, began applying first aid to the wounded but routine soon took over from her and she found that whatever she might have offered to help with was the responsibility of somebody else. She found paper and a pen, wrote out a statement in longhand, left it on Ian's desk and went home. The officers of the law seemed to have quite enough to be getting on with without having to nursemaid a young vet who was beginning to feel slightly sick.

Ian Fellowes was determined to remain on his feet and take over, but it was quite obvious that such a course of action would be likely to kill him. He was whisked away, protesting vigorously, to the cottage hospital. Being the nearest that he had to a deputy, DS Bright took over. He appeared at the front door of Whinmount just as dusk swept over the land. Roland, who had heard nothing of all this, made his appearance seconds later. The result was a period of babble during which Roland was asking questions, Jane was trying to answer them while explaining developments so far and asking a few questions of her own; and Bright, who was faltering under the weight of unaccustomed responsibility, was trying to explain, report, reassure and answer questions without drawing breath.

When a sort of calm had been restored and Jane had managed to get the small group seated in the kitchen with mugs of tea, Bright reviewed his report which, stripped of irrelevancies, boiled down to this: 'God alone knows where that young madwoman's got to. I've had every man and woman I could raise scouring the woods and empty buildings and there's no sign of her, none at all.'

'Did you tell them to keep looking up?' Jane asked. 'She's a climber, remember. I told Ian Fellowes. It's human instinct to flee upwards but searchers hardly ever look up.'

'Was I in the room when you told Mr Fellowes? But never mind it for now. The leaves are still on the trees so it would be easy enough to hide yourself among the branches of a big hardwood, and now the light's gone. From what she was saying, it's you she blames for her downfall and I'm damn sure it's you she's coming after. Short-handed as we are, we could never cover the whole area and we'll have to use a few men to cover the railway and the bus stops in case she makes a run for it. Do you think she'd know how to steal a car?'

'For a while,' Jane said, 'about two years ago, she was very much in love with Duggie Gough.' Young Gough had been a prominent local car thief, now believed to be in Canada but still pursuing the same profession.

'And now she's been going around with another mechanically-minded young yob,' Bright said gloomily. 'The question is, does her hatred of you outshine her wish to escape; and on the whole, going by the look I saw on her face, I would say probably yes. Anyway, I can't take any chances. Is there anywhere you can go, anyone the pair of you could possibly go and stay with a long way from here, where you'd be safe for the night? Obviously you must tend your patients tomorrow.'

Jane might have shrugged off the threat from Helen Maple, but Bright, usually the most stolid man in the tradition of British policemen, was obviously nervous and he communicated his nerves to Jane, who began to feel a fluttering of her insides as she explained that Roland's parents were in New Zealand and that her own were dead.

'Then all I can do,' said Bright, 'is guard you as well as circumstances allow. I've phoned Edinburgh and Honeypot promised that she'll send every man who can be spared . . . in the morning. Same story all round. Scraping the bottom of the barrel and working the men in shifts, I reckon I can keep watch on the main road and the car parks and put a warning out to the bus company. That'll leave me four men in or near this house during the night. That's one man near each door plus one outside this room.

And that includes me. Not a lot to fend off a madwoman, especially one who's a skilled climber and a bit of an athlete, by all accounts. Tomorrow, if we haven't caught her, we'll see about finding a safe house for you. Maybe your sister in Dublin . . .'

Jane made a face. She had largely overcome her dislike of her sister but their childhood hatred still waited in the background, ready to erupt at the first careless word, and her acceptance was not reciprocated.

Neither Mr nor Mrs Fox felt like doing any useful work during what was left of the evening. Bright would have been seriously hampered in making and maintaining his dispositions if the householders had been pottering about the place. An early night seemed to be called for. Happily, each was immersed in a lengthy book at the time – Jane in a new treatise on veterinary practice and Roland proofreading Simon Parbitter's latest crime novel. Thus occupied, they found that the time passed swiftly.

Jane, whose habit it was to sleep in the nude, rose once before turning out the light and wrapped herself in a towelling bathrobe with a dressing gown over the top in order to make tea and to dispense biscuits to the officers on guard duty as well as to Roland and herself. The night had become hot and stuffy, so that to have attempted to sleep in those unaccustomed gowns would have been wasted effort but Jane, remembering the likelihood of there being a man on the landing, hung them carefully behind the door. She often had to rise in the night.

The night was also very still. When the lights were out and they were trying to settle, Jane said, 'Roley, are you afraid?'

Roland was fairly sure that any reply suggesting that Helen was *only a girl* might be taken amiss. 'I'd be nervous,' he said, 'except that it's not my job to be nervous. It's Sergeant Bright's job to keep her well away from you and me and I don't see what I can do to help.'

'I can't think of anything very practical,' said Jane. 'In a way, that's what scares me. Whenever I'm doing something useful that contributes to our safety, I'm never scared; but waiting for somebody else to protect me, that's terrifying. We don't know how good Sergeant Bright will be at the job.'

'I can understand that, I think. Would it help if I got out your shotgun and had it ready?'

Her whisper came out of the darkness. 'That would be waiting for somebody else to act. And you're not used to it. Nor are you licensed to handle it. If you fired a shot with policemen all around there might be hell to pay. But if you gave it to me with a couple of shells, that might help. The law would allow me to fire a shot if I had good reason to believe that my safety or my possessions were being threatened.'

Roland sighed, not so much at the thought of getting out of the warm bed but more at having to detach himself from a warm and naked Jane. He switched on his bedside lamp and quitted the bed. Jane's shotgun was one of her several bequests from her great-grandfather. It was an old gun but of very high quality by a top maker.

With only one gun in the house, the police had accepted that a solid oak built-in wardrobe reinforced by a digital lock would be acceptable security. In addition, the wardrobe was, as usual, so full of clothes that the gun was not immediately obvious. Jane had some idea of the value of a top class hammer gun from the 1870s by Westley Richards and had had to stop Roland airing his damp laundry on the barrel. He found and extracted the gun and took it to Jane, handing her a brace of orange cartridges separately.

Jane loaded the barrels and laid the gun beside her right leg. She knew full well that a hammer gun, not having a safety catch, should not be cocked until the moment before firing; but that moment can be an eternity when danger threatens. She cocked both hammers. Then, comforted by the familiar feel of the comb, the action and the trigger guard under her hand, she pulled the single sheet up and fell immediately asleep.

TWENTY-TWO

Jane was jerked awake an hour later by a hubbub on the landing. The second that it took for consciousness to dawn allowed the confrontation to develop. Jane's eyes opened on an appalling scene. A gibbering madwoman was arriving at the foot of the bed. Her hair, threaded with leaves, was flying wildly and she was screeching threats beyond comprehension. A subsequent enquiry tracked her route through the downstairs lavatory window and up what had once been the shaft for a dumb waiter to the upstairs landing before her presence had been detected, but Jane knew nothing of that. Of Roland, who had gone to answer a call of nature, there was no sign.

Helen was still brandishing the knife clotted with dried blood, completing a spectacle that was awe-inspiring enough to cause the few officers present to hesitate for what might have been a fatal second. To Jane, in those first fraught seconds, they seemed a crowd but not a useful crowd. In an instant of panic she clutched the shotgun, lifting the muzzles and pulling both triggers.

The consequences followed a predestined path. The hammers came down on the strikers which in turn struck the percussion caps. The styphnate in the percussion caps fired small spurts of flame into the nitro powder. About fifty grains of nitro powder sent just over two ounces of lead shot on its way. The shot passed close over Helen's head and blew a hole in the wall just below the ceiling. Her head was below the line of the shot but it was in the path of the sound and shock wave.

Stunned by the blast, she nearly poked her own eye out as she brought up her hands in a defensive gesture. Instead, she jabbed herself in the forehead. Any lingering clarity of thought went by the way. In a monumental explosion of fury she hurled down the knife, pinning her own left foot to the floor by the web between the first and second toes.

Now that she was no longer holding the knife, the four policemen who had been hampering each other by crowding with Roland through the bedroom door were encouraged to grab her by the wrists. Before taking any further action, however, they were frozen to the floor by the final outcome of the two shots. The amount of gas generated by those two shots was not great. Cold, it would have been of no great significance. Propulsive powders when fired expand, cold, by a factor of at least six thousand, but they leave the muzzles at a very high temperature. Thus the volume was very much increased, quite enough to fill the space beneath the sheet. The single sheet was wafted well on its way towards the ceiling where it hovered, much like a giant stingray in a sub-ocean film.

Jane rolled over on to her face and, not for the first time, prayed for the gift of invisibility. She could only give thanks that, this time, there were no cameras clicking and flashing as they recorded her shame for posterity.

EPILOGUE

A few months later, around the time of Helen Maple's court case, Jane and Roland welcomed a little baby girl into Whinmount after a particularly long and arduous labour. The run-up to the trial and the necessary rehashing of witness statements and evidence had been rather eclipsed by this happy event, but on the day when Jane was expected to give her evidence in person, she was there, with special permission to leave the courtroom every three hours during her testimony – should it last that long – and go and feed her ravenous daughter. Roland had come into his own since the birth of Gilda and taken over the general day-to-day caring for her during the trial. There were even discussions between Jane and Roland that he would become the full-time carer and stay-at-home father . . .

The trial over, Helen found guilty of murder and several counts of aggravated burglary and in prison for the next ten years at least (surely her anger wouldn't allow her to be released early for good behaviour) life could try and get back to some semblance of normality once again. Jane's veterinary practice was flourishing, Roland's novel was on hold whilst he spent most of his time looking after his daughter and taking on other roles to do with the running of their household – all very much to everyone's surprise, including his own!

Ian Fellowes got over his injury fairly swiftly and sent everyone at the station on a self-defence course in case they should be faced with a mad knife-wielding woman ever again. And poor Alistair Ledbetter continued to pursue and refine his gambling habit and never did learn his lesson in either the women he chose as partners nor how to live within his means.